Three
Chestnut H

OTHER TITLES IN THE SERIES

Three Chestnut Horses

Margita Figuli

Translated by John Minahane

Central European University Press

Budapest ● New York

English translation © 2014 John Minahane

Published in 2014 by

Central European University Press
An imprint of the
Central European University Limited Liability Company
Nádor utca 11, H-1051 Budapest, Hungary
Tel: +36-1-327-3138 or 327-3000
Fax: +36-1-327-3183
E-mail: ceupress@ceu.hu
Website: www.ceupress.com

224 West 57th Street, New York NY 10019, USA
Tel: +1-732-763-8816
E-mail: meszarosa@ceu.hu

ISBN 978-963-386-054-0
ISSN 1418-0162

"This project has been funded with support from the European Commission.
This publication reflects the views only of the author, and the Commission cannot be held responsible
for any use which may be made of the information contained therein."

Library of Congress Control Number: 2014953620

On the cover:
Martin Benka: *Po búrke* (After the storm), 1918.
Courtesy of Slovak National Gallery.

Printed in Hungary by
Prime Rate Kft.

Contents

Introduction

An Evocative Story of Love and Horses

In 1918, at the end of World War I, the Austro-Hungarian Empire fell apart and the Czechoslovak Republic came into being. For Slovaks this meant the end of a threat to their national existence. The new situation enabled them very quickly to construct their own school system (until that time teaching at all types of schools could only be done through Hungarian) and to establish and develop such basic cultural institutions as theatres, publishing houses, artistic associations, galleries, museums, radio stations, and so on. There was all-round rapid development in culture and education during the period which followed. To no small extent, that affected Slovak literature in all its types and genres. Earlier, at the turn of the twentieth century and right up to the World War, it was as if authors had a "duty" to make the issues of national life thematic in their works. Literature was performing functions of enlightenment and writers also were to some extent engaged in politics, and so in the assessment of particular works the ideological position of the author was often more important than the actual aesthetics of the text. But now, at the war's end, new prospects were opening up for poets, prose-writers and dramatists. Of a sudden, the human person could be and must be portrayed not as the bearer of national affiliation but as an individual human being living his or her own fate, and marked not only by socio-historical circumstances but especially by private, intimate relationships, and by personal losses or failures.

Responding to the new situation, Slovak prose went through rapid changes during the 1920s and '30s. A contributory factor was the flourishing of translation, which made it possible to become acquainted with the major world classics and the works of living European authors. The programmatic aim, as formulated in various journal articles, was to open up to Europe, and what was understood by this was not simply drawing impulses from the literature of other nations but also seeking to bring domestic literary production nearer to the level of the finest works written in lands to the west of Slovakia.

Within a short time Slovak prose-writers widened the thematic focus in their stories, novellas and novels. The theme of city life, rarely addressed until then, came to the forefront. In a number of works the plot was located outside of Slovak territory, sometimes in exotic settings. Alongside war and social themes, issues of complex human interrelationships were developed. And in particular, the writers tried out a variety of artistic approaches: traditional realism enriched with satiric elements, detailed psychological sketches, expressionism, naturalism, surrealism, impressionism... A striking feature was the lyricisation of the epic text by a variety of means.

One of the peaks of these developments is represented by the work of four prose-writers, Dobroslav Chrobák, Ľudo Ondrejov, František Švantner and Margita Figuli. All of them situated their plots in the natural setting of the mountains, which they knew intimately. They made their appearance in literature roughly in the mid-1930s. Critics at first used the concept of *lyricised prose* to designate their work; later the term *prose of naturalism* became established in literary historiography. This was not, however, a literary group, that is to say a group of authors coming forward with a formulated creative programme. These authors wrote independently of one another. Nonetheless the experts distinguished certain common features in their work: depiction of an upland milieu, mythicisation of the mountains, characters living in symbiosis with nature and its bio-rhythm, accentuation of the struggle between good and evil, retardation of the epic action by lyrical means, ballad mood, dream atmosphere, and so forth.

Margita Figuli, the author of the book which you now, dear readers, hold in your hands, was born in 1909 in Vyšný Kubín, a village in the mountain region of Orava in Northern Slovakia. (Her remote ancestors had come from Italy, hence the non-Slovak-sounding name.) She completed her secondary schooling in the little town of Dolný Kubín and in Banská Bystrica, where in 1928 she gained her *maturita* (equivalent to A-level in Britain). Subsequently she took up employment as a clerk in the Tatra Bank in Bratislava, where mainly she dealt with correspondence in English. In 1939 she married the medical doctor Jozef Šuster, afterwards a university professor, with whom she spent forty one years (he died in 1980). They had one son, Borislav (1944), who later became the central figure in her memoir *Ariadne's Thread*. Previously, however, in 1941, the author had been dismissed from the bank. According to her own later testimony, the reason was that the fascist-leaning directorate of this financial institution disliked her opposition to the war waged by Hitlerite Germany, clearly expressed in her novella *The Leaden Bird*, which had been published in a journal. From then on she devoted herself professionally only to literature. She died in Bratislava in 1995.

Already by the mid-1930s, following the publication of a number of her prose pieces in various journals, Margita Figuli was perceived as a major talent by the literary community. Her first book *Temptation*, containing ten novellas and short stories, appeared in 1937. Three years later she produced her most famous work, *Three Chestnut Horses*, which evoked an unprecedented response among reading public and literary critics alike and, to put it figuratively, ensured her immortality. Further important works of hers include the extensive historical novel *Babylon*, the novel *Youth*, where the author's life experience in childhood and adolescence is mirrored, and the already-mentioned memoir with an essayistic tuning, *Ariadne's Thread*. A number of Margita Figuli's texts are unfinished, in sketches or fragments; these have remained the property of the family and are not accessible even to scholars. She also produced literature for children, radio plays, publicistic essays, and the libretto for a ballet. *Three Chestnut Horses* and *Babylon* have been translated into many languages.

When Slovaks of even a little education hear the name Margita Figuli, automatically the title *Three Chestnut Horses* resonates in their minds. Even those who have never read it know it in rough outlines. It is not only the author's most famous work but unquestionably one of the best-known works of Slovak literature. And since literary scholars too have assigned it among the prose works that receive exceptional attention, it is one of those products of art which are written about and interpreted most often. It is interesting, then, that to this day there is no agreement on the genre definition of *Three Chestnut Horses*. Some scholarly works refer to it as a novella; others call it a novel, or a short novel; there is even the hybrid designation of "novelistic novella". While for scholars the question of genre demarcation may be important, it may be quite insignificant, needless to say, for readers. The fact remains that when the work made its appearance in 1940 it immediately became a literary hit, a bestseller. Up until 1947, hence in the space of seven years, six further identical versions were published; such a number of editions of one and the same work in such a short space of time had never previously been known in Slovakia and was not to be repeated. Later on, admittedly, the work's existence, and its repeated introduction into the communicative circuit, was notably complicated. This had to do with the coming to power of the totalitarian communist regime in Czechoslovakia in 1948. That regime, as we know, by all available means suppressed religious faith and promoted atheism, and in

Three Chestnut Horses there are strongly religious passages (for example, right at the beginning the protagonist's inner monologue has the character of a prayer to the Lord). In subsequent years the work appeared – whether with the author's agreement or without it – with certain cuts and insensitive interpolations. So then, not every Slovak reader has read it in the form in which it originated and first saw the light of day. You, dear readers, are receiving it in a translation made from the original, undiminished exemplar.

A contributory factor, probably, to the enormous contemporary popularity of *Three Chestnut Horses* was the fact that it appeared when the chaos of war was sweeping through all of Europe and the foundations of faith in the goodness of man were being violently shaken. Margita Figuli offered her readers a pure and delicate story of love, where the characters were sharply drawn and the line between good and evil was distinct. Today's readers also may find to their taste the fast pace of the plot, the presence of characters who are gripped by passion, and not least the fact that the philosophy of life laying emphasis on morality and humanity is not codified in reflections by the author but emerges rather from the events depicted and the characters' behaviour. Though the author does not make use of extensive descriptions, nonetheless she manages to convey very evocatively, for example, the atmosphere of the mountains, whose beauty and mystery enchant the main character and through his perceptions the reader also. The attractiveness of this prose is increased by the treatment of the erotic motif, which tenderly twines, as it were, through the entire epic action, as do – to a lesser extent – the elements of adventure. One of the opening scenes, played out on the Slovak-Polish border, which involves an encounter between horse smugglers and men of the law, might have been taken from a Western. As a point of interest I may mention that the tradition of smuggling these noble animals from Poland to Slovakia and vice versa survived in the author's native region right down to the 1970s. Granted, by that time it was no longer done as a gainful employment but was rather a mark of prestige among maturing youths, a kind of adrenalin sport.

À propos the horses: the title signifies that they will play an important role. And in truth, apart from their actual presence in the plot, where the author has given them literally a fateful role, they are bearers of certain indirect, profound significances. Slovak literary scholarship has by now produced many pages on the symbolic layers of *Three Chestnut Horses*. I believe they have been retained in the English translation, and alert readers will discover them for themselves. They are important, because they turn what is at first sight a perfectly simple story, with something of a fairytale air, into a genuine masterpiece.

Igor Hochel

I.

I do not ask the Lord for worldly vanities, because wealth, profit and glory set man's heart on fire only for a joyful moment, and I want my heart to burn with joy eternal. I do not ask Him to sate me with happiness and joy that are not lasting, because I am on my way to the source of His living water, and there my thirst and my hunger will be satisfied. I do not ask that a sword be put in my hand, sharp enough to overpower my enemies; but rather that the Lord may keep my soul and body in readiness, guarding them as the apple of His eye; let Him rather hide me in the shadow of His wings, for blessed is he whose strength is in the Lord. And therefore may He raise me up, so that I may learn to walk in godly paths. May He cleanse my heart from the dust of the earth and fill it with immense goodness, so that I may serve my fellow-man well. May He preserve His sacred image in me, so that I may go with Him in the land of the living and praise Him. May He direct my reason with His most loving counsel, so that I may act justly among the just. In patience, faith and action may I be perfect and entire, lest my deeds be like the sand that is scattered by the wind. May my thinking be whole, because a man in two minds is like a tree split in half. May my thoughts not be conveyed in ambiguous, sly and deceitful words, but may my speaking be as a spring, giving rise to one pure stream.

So much do I ask from the Lord, who was the God of Jacob, and I want Him to be my God too, because His mercy reaches to the heavens, His truth is raised above the clouds, and His justice rises higher than the mighty mountains.

My head was full of such thoughts as I returned home in the early evening through the forest, dense as the dusk of December, for such are the woods in this region. I was making my way back on my chestnut horse and listening in the immense quiet of the mountains to the clinking of his hooves, which blended with the heavy, monotonous murmur of the trees. We had come from the borders through the hills, and our one companion had been the north wind, which was running through the canyons between the peaks, where it would rest during the summer's night.

Slowly it was growing dark, and at every moment I expected the sky to open up and the stars to appear. I guessed the places where each star would shine, and in the end I fastened my eyes on one particular spot, believing that one of them had to appear precisely there.

Proceeding onwards, I gazed at the sky and thought of a light that was like this star. I was thinking of the light of my youth, to which my thoughts always turned after my long journeys. That light was my beautiful Magdalena. I had spent my childhood with her in my native village in Turiec. To see her image in my mind I would travel back through the years and each time I would find it there, unchanged.

She is waiting for me, young and smiling at the threshold of her house, which neighbours upon our own. I run to her eagerly, we grasp each other's hands and, full of enthusiasm, we escape into the fields. We find a narrow path through the ripened rye and we go that way. Magdalena's hair, yellow as wax, is blowing on all sides. One blade of rye gets entangled there and I release it. Magdalena is a young girl who cannot yet understand love. But at that moment I become her swain, struggling with his first temptation. Disentangling this stalk from Magdalena's hair, I cannot but feel how delicate and soft it is, and I would like to plunge my face into it. The very thought of this delicious sensation excites me, but I do not dare. I postpone it to the time when Magdalena will be able to understand the meaning of these beautiful things. I must be content to take her hand and dash along with her further. With the sun at its warmest we return home, all out of breath and innocent and young.

Magdalena's mother emerges from the porch. Our hands unclasp under her strict gaze. Afterwards, round the corner of their house, while I'm standing close by, I hear how she scolds Magdalena for making friends with me. With a humbled heart I trudge away beside the wall towards our yard. Although I would prefer to cry, I grit my teeth, and my heart fills up again with courage.

Now, journeying on my horse among the peaks, I felt this courage still, and so with an equal courage I looked in the face of the star which just at that instant was peeping out from the clouds, right at the spot where I had been gazing. I do not know if I meant to say it to the star or if I meant to say it to God, Who reigns above her, but at that moment I said:

'I do not ask for worldly vanities, which make a man's heart blaze with momentary joy, but I ask, along with God's grace, one thing only, I ask for my Magdalena, because I want my heart to be on fire with joy forever.'

Indeed, at that time I had no other desire in the world than that I should ask Magdalena to be my wife, and that Magdalena would understand and would agree. A few days previously, when I set off among these peaks, I resolved that on the way back I would stop at her parents' place and ask her for her hand.

Magdalena belonged to my life, because without her my life was vain and desolate. Magdalena was the only immaculate power I believed in here on earth, as I believed in the immaculate power of God in Heaven. Therefore she was rightfully mine, and therefore I had chosen her above all women.

Although I had not seen her for quite a long time, that did not need to be an obstacle. We were linked by our childhood years and again by a new encounter five years ago in Turiec. She had seemed to me then so lovely, gentle, and good, that I dreamed of her as of a promised land. From that time onwards I had been thinking of her more and more, until finally I decided to set out for her region to ask her to be mine forever.

It happened that a convenient opportunity arose. I had to go to inspect some wood under Babia Mountain, which I had purchased for a sawmill in Žilina. On the way back I planned to stop in the village near the county town, where Magdalena's parents had kept a hostelry since migrating from Turiec. Now I wanted to sleep here, in the nearest outbuilding, and then, on the following day, I would carry out my purpose.

As I thought about it all my heart trembled, as a mountain trembles in the wind or the stars between the clouds that were above me now as I moved forward on my chestnut horse.

*

I'd been going from the Polish border towards lower Orava. Behind my back Babia Mountain was still jutting out, like the outward breathing of that hilly land, smoothed to a rounded shape by the bitter gales.

In the valley in front of me I spotted the first roof, with a cross standing out against the horizon. I did not know the name of the settlement which I could see beyond the church, but that was of no consequence. The important thing was that I would have somewhere to sleep and rest, worn out as I was from the day-long travelling.

Weaving my way between the spruces, I came to a clearing and I would soon have made out the way to the village, when something made my horse uneasy and fearful. I too became somewhat unnerved, and immediately I pulled on the reins to make him gallop. But my horse, instead of rushing off, stopped still, shivered, and cocked his ears. I spurred him sharply a few times in the underbelly, but he stood as if made of stone. Plucking up my courage, I looked around me to see if some danger was threatening.

At that moment two shots rang out from the Polish side and the echoes carried thunderously through the peaks. Immediately afterwards we were surprised by a loud noise which rolled down the mountain towards us like some gigantic boulder. It was approaching at such speed that I could scarcely keep track of it. All I could hear was twigs snapping and the earth shaking. Eventually I distinguished the drumming of hooves, and right then I spotted a team of seven horses careering through the trees. I knew immediately that these could only be smugglers coming from Poland with the customs guard pursuing them. There were two men. They had the horses tied together with thin ropes for halters. One of them was leading two horses and the other five.

I moved aside, as they were racing down the hillside in a furious gallop straight towards me.

The one in front was pressed right down upon his horse's back, to avoid the bullets. The man behind him was hanging in the stirrups with his face turned up to the sky. He appeared to be wounded.

My horse, in confusion, reared up, spluttered, and then took off along with the others, racing like a wild thing. I was quite unable to hold him back and had no other option but to loosen his bridle and gallop through the pasturelands at breakneck speed.

I guessed that the smugglers were making for the secluded wood behind the stream that flowed under Babia Mountain. They would have to hide so that our police would not catch them, and I too knew of this place as a safe refuge.

Two of us cleared the stream at a leap. Only the man hanging in the stirrups was left behind, because his horse shied at the last moment — afterwards it turned out that the animal had been shot through the thigh. In the end he laboriously jumped across the current, but he lost his footing on the slippery bank at the other side and fell heavily right on top of a sharp tree stump that ripped his belly open. The horse was still struggling when I went back to help his master. He looked at me so mournfully and beseechingly that I had to avert my eyes, because I pitied him so much. Indeed, I wanted to shoot him, but they wouldn't let me in case the shot gave us away. So we left him like that, at the mercy of the wild beasts.

Naturally, I first rushed over to free the lad who was hanging from the horse's body. His head was dipped into the stream and the water was lapping at his hair. I lifted him up, freed him from the straps, and laid him on the bank, on the grass.

He breathed, came to life and looked at me. I felt him staring, rigid with surprise. Slowly he opened his mouth and grasped my hand, saying:

'Am I dreaming, or is it you, Peter, really you?'

'It's really me,' I replied, and I too was amazed to find him here.

Now I can speak fairly calmly about this shock, but at the time my heart was pounding as if it would burst right through my breast. That was how agitated I was, because the man lying before me was none other than

Jožko Greguš from Vyšný Kubín, yes, Jožko Greguš, Magdalena's cousin.

Only a little while back I had begun weaving a story out of our two lives, Magdalena's life and mine. I thought no one else would enter that history apart from us, but I had barely taken a few steps when it all began to get tangled up. So I sensed that this encounter in the remote mountains of the Polish border could not be pure coincidence. Disquiet surged into me suddenly, like lightning striking a tall tree. The one who made me most uneasy was the one who had fled with the five horses, and involuntarily I spun round in his direction. By now he had the horses tied to trees and was looking down from the height at us where we were by the stream.

'Who is that man?' I asked Greguš suddenly.

'That's Zapotočný,' he replied absent-mindedly, running his fingers over his head to see if he was wounded.

'Which Zapotočný?' I pressed him, because there were many Zapotočnýs.

'Jano Zapotočný ... Jano Zapotočný from Leštiny,' he said eventually, rising.

'I've heard of him,' I remarked casually, wanting to know more.

'And well you might,' he said with relish, 'since he's the leading farmer in Leštiny and the most dangerous horse smuggler. He doesn't do that often, because he doesn't need to. He's got money like chaff. But now and then the passion seizes him. This time round he roped me in too, and I all but paid for it with my life. I won't be lured a second time, not if Poland had horses of gold. But this time I had to bend to his will, because he wanted to smuggle in a few more horses before the wedding. After that, according to him, he's going to give up smuggling and just be a farmer. He's still only at the stage of deciding to go and propose to her, but he expects he'll be successful at that. So he's decided that on the way back from these hills he will ask for her hand.'

'On the way back from these hills ...' I repeated mentally after him.

Mentally I repeated it after him, and I felt a mild shiver go through my body at the thought that a similar duty awaited me. Just that my situation would be more difficult, because I didn't have money like Zapotočný. I didn't have money like chaff. I didn't even have my own roof over my head. I was a common tramp who bought wood round the country. But this did not in any way deter me. That day I was so audacious and resolute that I had no fear of asking her to join with me forever. And I believed that my Magdalena would unite with me, because she would always prefer love to mammon, such a great, deep and pure love as my own.

I was musing like this all the time that Greguš was talking about Zapotočný. In the meantime we had taken our two horses and set off up the slope. We left the third horse on the bank, his eyes distracted, glazed by suffering. That was the one with the riven belly, and now he was dying. Once more I picked up my gun to shoot him, because his pain was eating at my heart like rust on iron.

Zapotočný, furious, shook his fist from the height, warning me not to dare shoot, for fear of alerting the policemen who were still lurking nearby. And he was right - we might easily have given ourselves away.

Greguš too eventually caught my hand. To divert me from my purpose he took up his narrative again, saying:

'Look, I ought to tell you who Zapotočný has chosen. It'll interest you, definitely. When you were children you were neighbours in Turiec.'

That indeed caught my interest and I fastened my eyes firmly to his lips. Or rather, what fastened them there was the foreboding that, at that very moment, I might receive a fatal wound. I waited, unspeaking, tense, for Greguš to pronounce the name, and yet that was the very thing that I feared.

Then Greguš said:

'My cousin Magdalena.'

At that I pulled the trigger, so that her name would vanish in the noise of the shot. I could not listen to it, because it went through me like a nail, hammered through the skull into the brain.

While the shot animal wheezed and my hand dropped, Greguš repeated once again, as if I had not understood on account of the noise:

'He has chosen my cousin Magdalena, and she's lucky.'

I was not able to fire again, to block out the sound of that beloved name, because up on the crest, over which the first stars of nightfall were gleaming, Zapotočný was savagely cursing me for using the gun despite his warning. I was forced to hear her name audibly and accept the blow that struck me on the first step to my dreamed-of eternal happiness. But I had no time to absorb what I had heard straightaway, since my shot really had brought danger upon us.

I had scarcely come to my senses when we heard dogs barking and the police approaching from the opposite side of the hill.

Zapotočný, with a smuggler's dexterity, untied his horses from the tree and gave the sign for us too to mount up and go off at a gallop. We set off in the opposite direction and went with such tremendous speed that there was no time even to look round to see what was happening behind our backs.

*

The police did not catch us by Babia Mountain, but it was only by a hair's-breadth that we escaped. The dog came running after us, giving them our direction by his barking. Fortunately, when he was trying to get in front of our horses Zapotočný hit him deftly with the thick end of a whip-stock, and he rolled over, stunned. From then on we felt safer, and the further we got from the borders, the more securely we sped along.

Meanwhile it had grown completely dark. We drove onwards only by the light of the sky, seeking concealment in the commons.

My horse was holding up well – he was a good racer. Greguš's too would have been able for more. But Zapotočný's horses were completely exhausted, having come all the way from Nový Targ. They were staggering with fatigue. We advised Jano to let them rest awhile, now that we were free of the main danger. But strange to say, he didn't even acknowledge our suggestion. To keep them going he whacked his heels into their bellies, then spurred them with the ends of his boots. When even that did not work, he took the whip-stock from behind his boot and began to thrash the horses so unmercifully that Greguš and I shouted at him, the veins standing out on our necks, to stop his cruelty. The worst thing was that the horses took fright and we had a hard job bringing them to a halt.

Finally, near Jasenica, he pulled on the animals' halters to calm them down. They did not refuse obedience: they stopped, but they were turning their heads fearfully to all sides, as if expecting a new rain of blows. But he did not beat them again. He thrust the whip-stock in behind his boot and looked around our hideout. Not far away there was an area of waste ground. It had tall bushes and he pointed us over to it.

It was not entirely a safe place, but while I was making up my mind to tell him, Greguš anticipated me.

He asked him:

'Are you planning to rest here?'

'You'll see right away what I'm planning,' Zapotočný answered, and even the darkness could not conceal how his brutal face lit up.

'This isn't the safest place for us to hide,' Greguš objected, 'we're very near the village.'

'That suits me,' and a smile spread out the length of his coarse jaw. 'I've an acquaintance here, I'll be off to visit her.'

I saw how that displeased Jožko and how his face contorted.

Zapotočný took no notice and continued in broad, lusty language, saying that no matter what the journey, he wouldn't pass her by. It would be a waste of a warm bed, a fine drinking session and his fill of food. The wayfarer had a right to such refreshment, after all. He guffawed into the night and smacked his lips, as if the taste of all that was on his tongue.

I did not involve myself in their talk, I was merely an observer.

Greguš hung his head and looked at the ground.

'What's up with you?' Zapotočný roared at him, when he saw he was silent.

'Nothing,' Jožko said quite calmly, 'I was just thinking of Magdalena ... tomorrow you're planning to propose to her, or have you forgotten her?'

'I'll be going to her tomorrow,' he said with a smile, 'but I'm giving tonight to Eva, and if she wants it, I'll even give her a son to remember me by. Now, understand,' he said menacingly, 'not a word to Magdalena! You'll admit yourself that I wouldn't be much of a man if I didn't say goodbye to Eva. She'd be waiting for me and heating the bed for nothing. All year long she was faithful to me and she hasn't been niggardly with her love. I don't know if Magdalena will equal her. But...'

He came to his senses and himself admitted that he shouldn't talk like that. When he was silent a moment, Greguš took the opportunity to reason with him. But all words were in vain, and only now did he admit that the reason he had thrashed the horses was so as to get here in good time and be able to spend the night with Eva.

Now, when that cuddly creature was at hand's reach, he would have to be crazy to pass her by.

Because Greguš didn't want to have to guard the horses in an exposed area, Jano decided to bring them with him to Eva. No one would see them in the dark in the enclosed yard. He instructed us, if we were afraid, to go on ahead. But only a little way, and he'd catch up with us. He fixed a spot where we were to wait for him if he happened to be late, in the commons area of the county town. We should not go to the Maliariks' place without him, because then they would know immediately there was some reason for his absence. He was anxious not to give himself away, as he didn't want to lose Magdalena. From tomorrow she'd be his, and a little chicken like her wouldn't be a bad exchange for Eva.

Greguš's jaws moved sharply, as he gritted his teeth at these shameful utterances.

Zapotočný was ready to go, but he hesitated and then came over to me.

Intensely he said:

'You too, there's something I want to say to you.'

'Yes.'

'Girls like to hang around good-looking lads,' he said warningly, 'now be careful that our paths don't cross.'

I stood directly in front of him and did not shrink from the fist that he slid in close to me. I looked at him directly and with courage.

'Meaning, I wouldn't want anyone meddling in my affairs at the Maliariks' place,' he continued with eyes bulging, 'because whoever he was, I'd slit his throat.'

With that, he leaped on the middle horse and went on down the boundary line to the gardens just above the village houses. We saw him stop in a hedged-in area and rap cautiously on a gate. In a moment a female figure, whom we could see only vaguely from a distance, by the light of the stars, ran out to open it and flung herself round his neck. And he too gripped her in a tight embrace.

'Let's go,' Greguš said, as if stunned by what Jano had done.

'Let's go,' I agreed, and I felt how deeply insulting this behaviour was to Magdalena, when he would soon be promising to be hers forever.

At that moment I felt strength flowing into me, and I thought that if needs be I would not be afraid to stand against the whole world for Magdalena.

As if wanting to comfort her, mentally I said, as I listened to our animals' hoof-beats:

"I would not be afraid to stand against anyone, or against the whole world, if I were sure you would accept my defence. I would resolutely bare my breast and hold it steady for the knife, if that would help you. I would not feel afraid if I had to fight for your sake even against a man as savage as Zapotočný.

"Surely my words have surprised you, lovely Magdalena, and you wonder at how I have changed since I was a child and how little my speech resembles the way I spoke then. But you see, Magdalena, it is true of me too that when I was a child I spoke like a child, understood like a child and thought like a child, but now I am a man I have put away childish things.

"And I am glad that I have matured and that strength has flowed into my limbs. There are mighty obstacles to be cleared from the path that leads to you. I have little time to do it, because to one of us, to Zapotočný or to me, tomorrow you must say the decisive 'yes'. I have no way of knowing who you will choose, and so I ask God to be merciful and to stand by me."

*

At dawn we arrived at the county town's common.

We came without Jano, though we had gone slowly the whole way so that he could catch up. When he did not appear, all we could do was wait at the agreed place, since we were not supposed to go to the Maliariks without him.

Tying our horses to trees, we sat down among the willows by the river. A thick mist lay everywhere throughout the valleys, and although the first light was breaking we could scarcely make out the immediate vicinity. For a long while we smoked continuously, eagerly waiting for the sun to appear, because we were chilled from the long night.

Greguš was the first to voice his unease, saying:

'I'm sorry I ever let myself be led into smuggling. Far from profiting, I've only done myself harm, because I paid for two horses and now I only have one. Actually Magdalena's mother, old Mrs. Mailiarik, desperately wanted me to go, just to sweeten her wealthy son-in-law to be, and I sacrificed myself. She craves him like a bee craves honey. It's true that he owns nearly half of the common in Leštiny and it wouldn't be easy to find his equal in wealth around there. But I don't know if it's good for Magdalena.'

Misery gripped me as he spoke, but I asked him purposefully:

'Why would it not be good for Magdalena?'

And I spoke to him like that, in a tone remote from my feelings, so as not to give the impression that I cared.

'He's rather brutal,' he said, musing and drawing the smoke in deep, 'he's rather brutal and I'm afraid Magdalena won't be able to bear it.'

'So then, she shouldn't marry him,' I advised, outwardly indifferent. 'Magdalena will find someone better if she waits.'

'Someone better,' he repeated, eager to contradict me. 'She'll never find anyone better because, as I told you, Zapotočný's weighed down with money. But what constantly bothers me is that nature of his, because, for all her cheerfulness, Magdalena is a sensitive girl. Her mother's the one who's pressing her most, though it's said that old Maliarik, her father, has no liking for this match. He takes Magdalena's part, and she too is wavering. But how I see it is…'

He hesitated, but after a moment he continued:

'It seems to me that she's wavering because in her heart she's waiting for you.'

I scattered the ash from my cigarette-end over myself with surprise, and after that I did not even hear the rest of what Greguš had to say, because I was hearing that one thing incessantly:

"She's wavering, because in her heart she's waiting for you ... Because in her heart she's waiting for you ... She's waiting for you!"

I could not sufficiently hide my joy at this and I did not even want to hide it, since I assumed that Greguš was on my side. I could feel a love-sick glow burning in my eyes and all the hollows around my mouth filling with hope. After all, it was only right that Magdalena should belong to me. I thought it impossible that Magdalena, with her angelic beauty and goodness, could belong to that savage.

Just when I was surest of myself, Greguš threw away his cigarette-butt and began again urgently:

'And just because I'm certain that she's waiting for you, I want you to promise me that you'll be indifferent and cold to her, so she'll finally be convinced you don't care about her. After that, she'll easily decide for Zapotočný.'

So that was how the land lay.

As it dawned upon me what Greguš was pressing me to do, he gripped my hand in his and insisted that I should promise to ignore Magdalena, and that if she attempted to interest me or to kindle my love, I would reject her. I must not ruin the joy of the Maliarik parents, who were marrying their daughter so well. The girls in all of Orava County would envy her such good fortune. It would not be wise or decent on my own part if I were to spoil her prospect of becoming a wealthy farmer's wife. It would not be wise because I myself could not replace all that. In fact, judging by appearances, I probably had no interest in marriage and preferred freedom and the roaming life. And therefore he would be glad if I came with them to the Maliariks and persuaded Magdalena that it was useless to wait for me. I must make it plain to her that I didn't have a roof to cover her head or property to support her. That I was a pauper and an unsettled man, because I had vagabond blood in me.

'In a word, you must hammer those stupidities out of her heart,' he concluded.

Had he even guessed that I would only surrender Magdalena at the cost of my own life, he would certainly not have spoken like this, demanding that I act against my conscience.

'So are we agreed, Peter?' and he squeezed my hand.

'Wait,' I said, 'just a moment ago you were troubled by his nature, and I don't like his behaviour either. A man who spends his last night before making his proposal with another woman is not worthy of Magdalena.'

'You're right, but tell me, which of us men is any better? So will you promise? Maybe afterwards Zapotočný can be useful to you. Don't forget he's rich.'

'I will not traffic with my conscience and betray human beings like Judas did Christ', I retorted, and I pulled my hand free of his as a sign of scorn and disapproval.

Afterwards we stood silent under the willows.

Just once Jožko tried to convince me that he hadn't meant any harm.

I didn't have time to answer him, because the sound of a horse galloping near the stream interrupted me. Both of us looked out through the branches and saw Zapotočný finally making his way back. But what struck us immediately was that he only had the horse he was riding.

He raced in between us, all red and sweaty.

'Where have you got the other horses?' Jožko went up to him instantly.

'That swine,' he swore savagely, 'informed on me to the police when I told her I was getting married and this would be my last visit. I was barely able to make a run from the room and cut one horse loose quickly, to save myself. The four others were left there, and they're gone forever.'

'Looks like this wasn't one of our good nights,' Greguš said sympathetically.

'All because of that swine,' Jano repeated, refusing to calm down.

To have something to say, I ventured:

'And a waste of beautiful horses.'

Jano spun round to face me.

'A waste,' he said forcefully, 'but I've been thinking. I could buy this one of yours from you. That way at least I could keep the Maliariks from knowing what happened.'

It wasn't my horse, so I couldn't trade with him. I had borrowed him from an acquaintance of mine, a farmer, and I'd have to give him back.

I explained that to Jano, but he took it as a false excuse and almost skewered me with a look.

'Hang yourself on him,' he snapped, cutting me off, adding that he'd remember my lack of good will.

Once more he ran his narrowed eyes over me, and then commanded us to mount up.

We did so, and when we were standing in file ready we noticed a curious thing: our three horses were all identical, as if made to one likeness. All of them had a beautiful build and a gleaming chestnut coat.

On these three horses we finally set off towards our meeting with Magdalena.

*

The sun was slowly rising above the peaks, which were still soaked in darkness. The power of the first sunbeam blessed the sky and opened the way to the dawn. The whole arc of space was filled with a clear light that poured over us and our three horses. Their coats glittered and grew lovelier in the daylight.

Beyond the river the county town showed in outline, and like two hands folding, the iron curve of a bridge could be seen over the steaming water. On the other side of the bridge was the village where the Maliariks had their inn.

The nearer we came to it, the more fiercely my heart beat, but I gave no sign of what I felt.

It was Zapotočný who changed instantly, as if he were another man. He put on an air of great importance as soon as we set eyes on the Maliariks' house. Although he was exhausted, he tensed like a string, thrust out his fat-upholstered chest, straightened his bent back, pulled on the halter to make his horse keep his head up, and moved backwards and forwards in time with the animal's pacing. He struck these and similar poses just to make an impression.

Greguš and I did not have Jano's braggadocio, and so we arrived more modestly.

The stamping of hooves called Maliarik himself to the window, and immediately he came out to open the gate.

A few nosey-parkers emerged from the inn, and no sooner had we jumped down from our horses than someone called out, struck by the fact that our horses were so much alike:

'Mind they don't get mixed up in the stables!'

Speaking just so as not to go numb with the constant waiting for Magdalena, I said quite unthinkingly:

'Indeed, we wouldn't want them getting mixed in the stables!'

I attached no importance to this, but it irritated Zapotočný. I sensed that he couldn't bear even the sound of my voice.

He was irritated all the more when Maliarik, beaming brightly, welcomed me almost with tears in his eyes and squeezed my hand. I gathered that the old man was debating within himself whether he should embrace and kiss me. Finally, he decided to bring me inside straight away.

Zapotočný was glaring angrily at me, and so I said:

'I'll be in, uncle, as soon as I've taken care of the horses.'

'But these two will do that; you come on in.'

'I'll see to the saddle at least,' I said in a very deliberate way, because Jano's eyes were flashing fire and I didn't want to start a quarrel.

'You come in, Peter,' and he pulled at my sleeves, 'I haven't seen you for a thousand years, and I can't wait to hear about how you're getting on these days in Turiec.'

With that, he turned to the two others and said:

'You too, hurry up and follow us when you've seen to the horses.'

Instead of nodding, Zapotočný swore and yanked one of the horses' halters. The horse was mine and I wanted to tell him not to treat the animal so roughly, but I gritted my teeth and went with Maliarik, who pulled me inside by main force. As we went he never stopped clapping me on the back and pressing my hand, as if he wanted to squeeze out all the moisture from the streams of Turiec and all the fragrance from that lovely land that might have lodged in the palm of my hand.

He ushered me into a very snug little room and told me it was Magdalena's.

A strange feeling ran through my body at these words and came back every time I thought: supposing she enters here now. I felt I would not be able to bear it, and that with my first glance at her I would turn into a pillar of salt, like Lot's wife when she turned round to look at Sodom.

Meanwhile, Maliarik had poured liquor into two small tumblers and invited me to clink glasses with him in token of welcome. We picked up our drinks and put them to our lips. I drank mine down straight away, because it would do me good after that foul night. But Maliarik, with the tumbler at his lips, was gazing piercingly at me and not drinking:

'What is it you find so strange, uncle?' I asked him.

'It's you,' he said, 'how you've grown, and how handsome you've turned out. I think our Magdalena will be surprised.'

Only then did he toss back his glassful, grimacing a little from the fiery liquor.

'Why would she be surprised?' I asked. 'Why would your ...' I wanted to say 'Magdalena', but for all the world I could not utter her name.

'Because she still imagines you as the boy who caught trout for her in the stream, who made her whistles from willow-wood, and who once in winter time climbed up a frost-covered tree to put a bit of grain for the little birds in the birdbox, and then fell down and broke his arm.'

These memories made me draw a deep breath, as if I wanted to smell once more the scent that remained in my hands from the last time I met her. And that was not just when we were children. Maliarik was mistaken, because Magdalena and I had met since that time, five years ago in Turiec, when she came to visit her acquaintances there. Evidently Magdalena had concealed this meeting from her parents, and I didn't know for what reason. But I had no time to puzzle the matter out, because Maliarik continued speaking.

He said:

'Magdalena and I often reminisce about you when we're alone. We recall your late parents too, and how they both lost their lives in that fire. When you were left an orphan, I tried to convince my wife that we should adopt you as our own. I always liked you. You were a good, upstanding lad. But my wife wouldn't agree. The poor thing, she couldn't help it, she was always thinking about money and she couldn't see her way to divide our fortune with a child who wasn't ours. But I was always glad to see you.'

'You talk like this, uncle,' I interrupted him, 'as if you want to make me burst out crying. But you won't succeed. My life has been tough and hard, and in a hard, tough life a man learns and unlearns all sorts of things.'

'I grant you that,' he nodded. He asked me how I had lived since the time they left Turiec, what I'd been doing and what I was engaged in now.

I was about to tell him that I factored wood for the Žilina sawmill, so I was roaming round the country. That same year we had also transported a good deal of bark for a leather factory in Mikuláš.

But I had scarcely begun when I heard the screech of a horse in the yard. I did not wait for more, because I guessed what must have happened. And sure enough, Zapotočný had just kicked my horse in the loins. I have no memory of how I left Maliarik in the room, where he'd been saying such lovely things, and found myself confronting Jano. I'd have taught him to treat animals decently if I hadn't controlled myself. Though I'd rather have sorted things out with him right there on the spot, I just pressed my lips tight and with a grim look let him know that he needed to take care. I wanted to avoid getting the pair of us known round the region as brawlers.

Afterwards I was so enraged that I did not even return to the room to join Maliarik, but just called to him through the window, saying we would talk later on. And indeed, there were customers in the inn whom he needed to serve, and we wouldn't have had much chance to enjoy each other's company.

Then I took the horse myself and tied him in the stable by the feeding-trough. Jožko's was there by the wall.

Zapotočný's was in the middle. My own was right out at the end.

And we left them like that.

We all returned to the inn, to refresh ourselves with food and drink.

There I finally learned why Magdalena had not appeared anywhere in the building and why my hungry and thirsty eyes had not been able to see her.

Early in the morning, before our own arrival, she had gone off with her mother to the meadows. They were haymaking at that time: the Maliariks had hay in Pod rúbaniskom. The two of them were due back home before sunset.

This meant I would have to wait the whole day before I saw her. But I was not afraid of that, because my love was patient, my love was self-sacrificing, my love endured everything, believed with constancy and waited in hope.

*

The sky grew overcast as I came back from the county town, where I had gone to pay farmers for wood I had purchased.

Rather than going first to seek Maliarik at the bar counter, I hurried straight to the stable to see my horse. I was fond of him, because he had a clear, agreeable look in his eyes and a love for human beings. This quality of his had immediately made me feel attached to him, as, on first meeting, you might feel attached to a woman you think is good.

I found Zapotočný in the stable. He started when I approached, because I'd caught him right at the moment when he was preparing to plunge his opened knife into my horse's leg. He'd have crippled him if I'd been a moment later. Embarrassed, he deftly sheathed the knife behind his boot. To deceive me, he gave me a twisted smile. But I do not let myself be fooled so easily and I said to him right away in plain language:

'That was to take revenge on me for not being prepared to sell him?'

He went red, grated his teeth and glared at me:

'Watch your lip!'

'I'll be watching the horse!' I retorted, furious.

'Better watch your neck, in case anyone sheds some of your restless tramp's blood!' he roared and took himself off with the knife-blade glittering behind his boot.

I had to restrain myself, or I would have hurled myself on his back and choked him on the ground. If the image of Magdalena hadn't risen before my mind, I would not have been able to stop myself from knocking him unconscious. But her clear, pure and beautiful form stood between us and averted misfortune.

I too made my way out, and on the threshold I looked round me again. My horse, too, at that moment swung his head round towards me, as if we had an understanding. Then I ran my eyes again over the other two, and once more I found they were all as similar as peas. It was just that my horse had the ends of his ears shaped quite differently to Greguš's or Zapotočný's. His were narrower, and above all at a more acute angle.

As I savoured the beauty of these three horses and especially my own, I heard Jožko Greguš calling me from the yard. I answered him, but immediately it occurred to me that Zapotočný had sent him on reconnaissance, to see if I was injuring his own horse. But he suspected me without cause, because I did not want to burden my soul with such dark deeds. And one more worry was buzzing in Jano's head: though the horses too mattered to him, what he feared particularly was that I might meet Magdalena alone. For safety's sake he had sent Greguš to stand guard. I did not want to inspire anger and misunderstanding, and therefore when he called me I answered:

'I'm coming. I just want to see if the horses have anything to eat. Maybe they could do with a handful of oats.'

'Just now we ordered exactly that.'

'That's fine.' I expressed outward contentment, but inwardly Zapotočný's voice was irritating me still, in that tone he used when he wanted to provoke me.

I moved then to follow Greguš. I was only about four steps behind him when suddenly I saw the fleeting movement of a head in the granary window, beyond the sheds. The head had ducked down, as if wanting to conceal the fact that it was gazing at us.

I felt I had to stop, though I didn't want to rouse any serious suspicion on the part of either Jano or Greguš. But then I grew angry with myself for this constant worrying about other people and I told myself: You're a man! What have you got to fear? And I stood still.

Greguš did not notice that I was not following him, and he strode ahead. I saw him once more as he entered the porch that was next to the inn.

Right at that moment I heard the lid of the corn-chest in the granary banging shut and a girl rushed out as if she was anxious to see me.

*

I knew her at the first glance.

It was Magdalena, and the fact that she was suddenly standing before me out of the blue left me incapable of moving, even though I had coped calmly enough with even greater surprises.

My throat was filled with her name and I wanted to utter it. But my heart was beating rapidly and, fearing that my voice might break, I instead took off my hat and greeted her silently.

'Peter!' she was the first to speak, but haltingly, and in a whisper, as if she had made me out from a distance and through mist, or as if she could not believe that it was really me.

To assure her that it was, I said:

'Magdalena, Magdalena,' and I came over to her. I did not take my eyes off her, and to this day I can still see her image clearly before me as it was at that moment.

She was holding two small buckets of oats in both hands and immediately I realised that they were for our horses. Her arms were uncovered to the elbow and she shifted her weight slightly from one foot to the other, her legs bare to the knee. On a finely developed figure her dress, coloured blue with white dots, fluttered in the breeze. The hem of her skirt was ornamented with a broad ribbon of diverse colours. A white tulle shawl was

tied crosswise over her breasts. I could see that the colour of her dress was the same as that of the evening sky
and of her own eyes. Set against the bright yellow of her
hair, the regular dark curve of her eyebrows arched over
those eyes, making a lovely pattern on her face.

But it was the eyes themselves that were the most
splendid feature. Even in childhood her eyes had been
captivating. But such was their beauty now, it was a
wonder I did not lose my mind.

She gave me her hand, softly half-closing her eyes,
and said in a joyful but nonetheless restrained tone of
voice:

'Good day and welcome.'

'Good day, Magdalena,' I said in a voice now steadier,
taking hold of the tips of her fingers.

I sensed that at that moment she too was lit up like a
candle.

I had nothing to hide from her, and so I gazed
openly into her eyes. But she suddenly flinched under
my gaze and drew her eyelashes shut, as if wishing to
preserve their mystery.

But all the more distinctly I understood what her eyes
contained. One thing only: that for all that time she had
been thinking of me, that for all that time she had been
waiting for me in her heart and in her mind, just as
Greguš had said. And she needn't be ashamed of that,
because I too had been waiting like her and I had believed with the pure faith of a child in this encounter.

Seeing everything so clearly, I began the conversation:

'Well, Magdalena, what a stroke of chance, that we
see each other again!'

First she nodded to me tenderly, but then she immediately corrected me:

'It isn't chance, Peter,' and she grew thoughtful, 'it had to be so. It had to be so, because something frightful would have happened,' and her face lengthened strangely as the smile disappeared.

'You want to tell me about something sad,' I felt it in her voice, 'but you must say more, because I don't understand at all.'

She looked at me, frightened, as if she had just been woken up, and all the softness vanished from her eyes. But then, apparently wanting to return to her normal state and to cover over what she had said, she tried to persuade me I was mistaken.

'There's nothing at all, Peter,' she said, forcing herself to smile. 'I just went off to give some oats to the horses, as my cousin Jožko requested. But see,' and she showed me the almost empty buckets, 'I haven't got them filled, because I came rushing out of the granary... and all on account of you, Peter.'

Those words "on account of you" ran through me like a fierce torrent, but I did not let anything show.

'Yes, and?' I pressed her further.

'And now I'm going to feed them, Peter,' she concluded, and, almost desperately, she tore her eyes away from me.

'What's wrong, Magdalena?' I asked her directly and openly.

She did not reply.

'I thought that you'd welcome me happily and be smiling...'

'Peter!' she interrupted me, and to hide the tears that were welling up in her eyes uncontrollably, she turned and fled to the granary.

What could be troubling her?

I went after her, and with one foot on the threshold and the other still on the step, I began to talk to her.

Swiftly she opened the lid on the corn-chest and with one cupped hand began throwing oats into the bucket which she was pinning with her elbow under her armpit. I saw how, now and then, a tear would fall among the grains. After that had happened several times, my heart grew heavy. I had known Magdalena as a girl full of courage and I knew it was no trivial reason that would compel her to weep. But she seemed to be afraid to explain her strange behaviour.

I therefore stepped towards her, and as she was bent over the corn-chest I caught her from behind with both my hands.

She started, and in fright she dropped the bucket.

'Magdalena,' I said, and I felt that this touch had caused my voice to change.

And even though I did not wish to do anything that would injure her beauty or goodness, I could not prevent myself from putting my arm firmly round her.

'No, Peter, no,' she responded.

'But yes, Magdalena, you must tell me what is troubling you. And there is no need to resist, for you must know that is all I want from you. Nothing else,'and I found the courage to say, 'my Magdalena.'

She trembled in my arms at those two words like a small flower when you breathe on it.

'Magdalena,' I told her without pausing, 'I want our meeting to be joyful, and therefore everything between us must be clear. We have not seen each other for years and years, but in my mind I have always been near you and I hoped that in your mind too you would always be near me. Was I mistaken, Magdalena? If it was not so, then I know that my hands must not touch you and these legs of mine, which had found the path to you, must find another path and leave you again.'

I said this with feeling and she may have decided at that moment to trust me with the full story, but no sooner had she lifted her head than we heard footsteps in the yard. Magdalena's mother, carrying the hay-makers' lunch-bag, had returned from the meadows. She could easily have spotted us where we were, and so Magdalena drew her head back from the window and straightened up; this obliged her to press closer to me. Immediately I too remembered how her mother used to discourage our meeting, so I too stood as if made of stone, not moving even an eyebrow. We looked after her, to see if she would cross the yard, and I noticed she was less energetic than in Turiec. But even so one could see she'd kept her hard, domineering nature.

Mounting the steps, she looked over towards the granary but did not notice us. She merely grumbled:

'Who left that granary door open? I'll have to go and shut it.'

And she took a step forward in our direction, but then decided she would first take the lunch-bag to the kitchen.

We had no choice but to separate.

Magdalena hastily indicated that we could meet later on. She determined the time and place: by the apiary in the garden, at nine in the evening. There she would tell me everything, but as she spoke tears came into her eyes again.

After that I left her, and she set about finally filling the buckets and bringing them to the horses. I walked as if I was bent under some sort of heavy load, as if I was carrying the Maliariks' house on my shoulders, and my head was splitting like mountain chains in an earthquake. In that condition I would have to wait until nightfall, but with God's help I would surely be able to manage it.

In the meantime dusk began to fall and blood spilled out over the western sky.

*

Time passed quickly and nine o'clock was approaching.

I stood by the apiary and waited for Magdalena.

My head was propped against the swollen bark of an old apple tree. Its fluttering leaves fanned my forehead, and their shadows flickered over my face in the moonlight.

My eyes were fastened on the path by which she would have to come. I could see her already in my mind: how her hands would be tucked under a muff, because it was rather cold. I saw the dew she had caught from the grass sparkling on her legs. I saw how, even far off, she wanted to smile at me, and at the same time tenderly lowered her eyes as women do.

I could not let go of her image even for a moment. I would go back to childhood and return again, and so compare what she was then with what she was now. The more I thought of her, the more I was yearning for her. I waited impatiently for her to be next to me and for the moment when I could finally ask her to be my wife. I didn't know how she would receive my words, but I was determined, because I had no reason for hesitating. I had never thought to say that to any other woman and there would never be anyone I would prefer over her.

If she understood me and if she agreed, then I would take her in my arms and carry her past the garden into the fields, where the rye stalks were swaying. I would pull a few blades and tangle them in her hair. Then, all excited, I would disentangle them again, and as she leant on my shoulder I would whisper words to her, so that she would understand the meaning of all those beautiful things I had hidden from her in youth and postponed to a later time. That time had now come, as the harvest time comes, or the time of ripening fruits, or the time of the buds' unfolding, or springtime or summertime. This time belonged to us, and I had lived to see it so that Magdalena would be my companion forever.

*

Everything was so beautifully prepared. Now all I needed was that she should come.

Suddenly I heard a cry from the yard.

Without hesitating a second, I ran down the garden. In the yard I saw nothing and everything seemed as it should be in the late evening dark. Could it be that I was mistaken? I thought it strange that this cry had not alerted anyone else. Admittedly the yard was spacious, with the outbuildings well distanced from the inn and the Maliariks' dwelling house, so that maybe those inside might not have heard.

I looked all round and considered what might have happened and where. Then the mournful cry was repeated, and at the same time there was a burst of neighing from the horses and the stamping of their hooves.

With a few bounds I had got as far as the stable. I literally flew in through the door and rushed over to our three chestnut horses.

A lantern was hanging over the little window, so everything could be seen plainly.

The horses were frightened, whinnying, rearing, and scraping with their hooves. Jano Zapotočný's horse had his mouth covered in foam. Greguš's was trembling and tugging at its chain. My own had his front leg raised, and when it saw me, it looked at me with such a gaze as if it had been changed into a human being. It was both sorrowful and imploring, and even betrayed some sign of gladness that I had come. That I had come just in time to save *her*.

It was Magdalena. She was lying under the horses and her head had fallen right under my own horse's hoof. The good fellow, he had carefully held his hoof over her face and prevented himself from letting it down. If Magdalena hadn't been my first concern, I would have liked to throw my arms round his neck and press his powerful neck against my chest, in gratitude that he had not crushed her beauty. But now my first thought was to save Magdalena.

36

I shoved Zapotočný's horse aside and caught her in my arms. My first thought was to carry her to her mother. But then it occurred to me that we had hoped to meet by the apiary and that there she was to tell me what was troubling her. Maybe I myself could bring her round and then speak to her as I had planned. Because I certainly would not be able to close my eyes that night until I had learned how things would be between us.

I brought her under the lantern and made sure that she was breathing. Her breath came heavily, but peacefully. She was unconscious and lay inert in my arms. Behind the door I noticed a pallet and I laid her on it.

I looked round the stall for a tub of water, but all I could see were the overturned buckets and scatterings of oats on the floor. Doubtless she had dropped them when one of the horses plunged and struck her.

I found no water, and so nothing else remained for me but to revive Magdalena with words.

I bent over her face, pale as the face of Christ taken down from the cross, and softly I called:

'Magdalena.'

There was no sign that she had heard.

'Magdalena,' I repeated more loudly, but I was afraid that someone might hear me and prevent me from speaking to her more.

I made the same attempt many times, but each time I was aware only of my enormous incapacity. Whatever I did, it was useless and in vain. At last I took her again in my arms and, feeling as if I were losing her forever, I took her to her room and to her mother.

The sound of talk and the clinking of tumblers reminded me again of Zapotočný, sitting there with his big bear's paws and broad jaw. How he would be sitting there with Greguš and preparing to make his proposal. All of that made me resentful and reluctant, but I had to act like a man and instead of taking her under the apple tree by the apiary, I brought her in God's name to her bed in her room.

When her mother saw her, she almost fainted. I scarcely knew who I ought to help first. What I wanted most was that she wouldn't make a scene, since I still hoped I would be able to speak to Magdalena alone. I had to tell her of my intentions before Zapotočný asked the family for her hand. But while I was placing her on the bed, her mother ran off to the bar room and screamed for help.

Immediately her father, Zapotočný and Greguš crowded in. All the customers of the inn were pressing behind them.

'You're not needed here,' I said sharply, slamming the door on the outsiders.

Now that we had only ourselves in the room, I asked the father to bring a little wine. Zapotočný looked at me as if he would gladly pound me to pulp. But I took no notice. I knew only that I had to save Magdalena, and that was what I was doing. He would have liked to push me away from the bed. But when the wine was brought, it was obvious that he didn't know what to do. I therefore took the glass in my hand, wet a piece of cloth in it, and dabbed all of her face. Her mother then undid the buttons on her dress and I moistened her throat and part of her chest with wine.

At last she opened her eyes.

Zapotočný immediately craned over her, but she drew her head aside. When her heavy, weary gaze discovered me, she let her eyes rest on me for a long time, as if she wanted to tell me she was grateful and impressed by the care I had given her.

'Magdalena,' her mother screeched unmercifully when she noticed, and she signalled to her behind Zapotočný's back not to look at me, because Jano would have second thoughts about the proposal.

But she gave no heed to the warning. She continued gazing at me and beseeching. Beseeching me to save her.

Again the thought came to me: why had I not carried her off into the fields and from there on into the moonlit night? I was certain that in such circumstances she would have agreed. But now it was too late.

Indeed it was, because Zapotočný asked Magdalena's mother to send me outside, since he wanted to speak to them about something important. I could not refuse such a command in a stranger's house. Even though I was sure that the principal matter was now impending: the proposal. I had not been able to forestall it, but I was able to hope that Magdalena's heart would never respond to Zapotočný's advances.

That was my single-minded belief as I left the room, hearing her mother instruct me further that I should wait in the inn until she could prepare a place for me to sleep.

*

No prospect was ever so daunting to me, I think, as to sit in the inn then and sprinkle my insides with wine. Nothing was ever so repulsive to me as to hear the merriment of others, while at the same time choking on my own grief. At that moment I would have thought it murderous for someone to force me to stay between four walls, where I would be deprived of fresh air.

And so I did not do as Mrs. Maliarik bade me, and I set off up, and then down, the village. I wandered among the houses and the people, carrying Magdalena's room in my thoughts and what was happening there just at that moment. I sought some means to relieve the uneasiness of my body and to find some calm. Unthinkingly, I set off down a track and found myself in a neighbouring village. From there I made my way back and went right through the county town and up the main road as far as Vyšný Kubín. In the end I took a detour through the fields and came all the way back again. My legs could have carried me no further, and when I found myself once more on the bridge linking the county town with Magdalena's village, from weariness I leaned against the railings and let my head hang over the water. Behind me the last carts were trundling along the road with sand and stone for some building site. Their heavy reverberation shook right through my soul.

From both of the town's clock towers came the harmonious beating of the hour, and the sounds carried over the roofs of the houses. Maybe my heart was beating no less audibly, but I smothered it, pressing it against the metal girder of the bridge.

An entire flock of clouds gathered above the river, recalling an image from my youth. That memory came at a good time, because it helped to deaden the torment in my mind, at least for a little while.

It was something that had happened at home, on the upland meadows.

Nightfall was approaching, and we were preparing for bed. Uncle Bad'o had laid the last coals on the fire. I stayed out for a while in front of the cottage, so as to welcome in solitude the darkness that brought us sleep after every scorching, exhausting day. I shut my eyes and wanted to feel it touch me. Suddenly something warm breathed on my neck, and my skin crept. I spun around and found a deer standing behind me. We had one that was tame. His head was turned upwards and he was looking all agog at the sky, as if seeing a miracle. He had wildness in his eyes, like a man in passion. I was curious to know what could have so astonished him, and I looked up.

The wind was rustling through the spruce twigs, and low above us it carried a cloud, light and airy, as if on a stallion's back. This white, pure and tender cloud had the beautiful form of a woman, lying in peaceful surrender in the wind's embrace. It carried her off to enjoy the quiet of night with her somewhere in the deep forest beyond the peaks, and so it vanished from our sight.

I understood the deer's longing, and I followed the wind's departure with hungry, jealous eyes. I too wanted to be borne over the mountain and, in the hollow of my hands, to find her whom I carried within me, as a man carries within him his heart. Since then I have often thought about that evening and felt how something momentous was filling my soul: the image of a woman who resembled that cloud and was called Magdalena.

That evening my wish should have come true, it seemed, when I bore her away from under the horses' hooves.

In reverie, leaning on the bridge's rail, I seemed to be standing in the stable under the lantern and holding her in my arms.

Her face was pale and pressed against my hip. Now I thought she was even more beautiful, and in my embarrassment at being so close to this beauty I was at a loss. I was like a child with the toy he had long desired given into his hands, but now that he has received it, in his surprise he doesn't know what to do with it. When I came somewhat more to my senses, the first thing I felt was fear and the dread of losing her again. As if there was someone at that moment who really did want to fight me for her, I pressed her to my body and I felt my veins seething, and a frightful strength coming into my hands. I would not give her up for anything in the world, because she belonged only to me, as my eyes belong to me, or my breath, or my blood, things to which no one else had any rights.

Saying all that to myself, I thought of Jano Zapotočny. And when I imagined that he would ask for her, that they would give her to him and that she would be his wife, it was worse than if Jano Zapotočny was choking me with his huge rough hand around my throat.

Everything might have been different if I had not brought Magdalena back to her room because it was necessary to revive her. But that is the way it is, when a man does not want to cease from walking on godly paths.

I wavered briefly, though, as I stepped through the stable door, holding her in my arms.

I could see a stretch of sky, full of stars, and beneath them the peaks that dominated this land. My eyes passed over one peak, a second and a third. Between the first and second peak there was a valley, covered in the bluish darkness like a soft bridal quilt. That was where I should take her, as that wind had carried its companion. There I should spend a peaceful night by her side. Then the dawn would wake us and for the first time I would appreciate that great fact, that Magdalena had become my wife.

It seemed to me I was going to do all that, and once again I could feel a boundless power in my body. At that moment too I felt the happiness that always coursed through me whenever I looked into her face.

Not far off I could see the back gate into the garden, and I actually took a step towards it. But then she seemed to open her eyes and look at me in a way that threw my head into a whirl. I knew that she did not want me to lose my mind. On the contrary, she wanted to bring me to my senses.

She wanted to tell me:

'What do you want to do, Peter? Don't you see how pure and innocent I am? Don't you see the purity and innocence in me? And you, when I long to be yours, do you want to defile me like a villain?'

That word *villain* was decisive and I became conscious of the sinfulness of my thoughts. But I was conscious of one thing more: if not today, then maybe never. And there, in pain, in hard, manly pain, I clasped her to my bosom.

I decided I would take her to the room, to her mother. But I also decided to take her to the garden and thence away between those two peaks. Although both were within my power, I had no great determination to do either.

In this state of indecision, I stood beneath the sky, beneath the stars. Around us was that frame of dark-blue mountains, lighted by the moon. And from out of the stable, my chestnut horse breathed on the nape of my neck, like the musing deer that evening before the cottage. My throat grew parched and I swallowed drily.

Mulling these things over, once again standing at the rail of the bridge that links the village with the county town, the river running underneath it and swaying like a strip of rye, I felt the hand of the watchman on my shoulder. Doubtless he found it suspicious that I'd been standing there so long without moving. Maybe he was afraid I was contemplating suicide. He sent me away and I obeyed, to free him from having to worry about my life. I did not explain to him that I could not die so long as my Magdalena was alive.

*

Coming back to the inn, I ran into Greguš in front of the gate. He had a bottle of plum brandy and two glasses in his hands. Young men were leaving the inn, singing merrily, and Greguš was giving them one for the road home. When he spotted me, he immediately poured a glass and offered it. He was far gone himself.

'Drink,' he directed me in a commanding tone of voice, pouring himself glass after glass, as if he had too little time for all the drinking he needed to do.

'I can't drink.' I refused because I felt no merriment; quite the contrary, misery gripped me ever more tightly by the throat.

'Go on, drink,' he kept pressing me, mercilessly. 'Tonight I could knock over mountain peaks for joy.'

'Not me, brother.' Although I was sad, I gave him a forced but genuine smile.

'Why not? You're sad because you're not drinking. Plain to see you're a stranger and you're not familiar with our ways.'

'I know my own self,' I replied, 'because if I drank I'd surely kill someone. I have to be careful.'

And I thought again of Zapotočný. Of the white bed, and of white Magdalena. And I imagined a similar bed, dressed as a bridal bed. And those paws of his overpowering her and taking what had been destined eternally for me. I ought to demand my right. I ought to remove him by whatever means. Really and truly, even kill him.

'Then you're a dangerous man,' Greguš told me, but he didn't grasp what I meant.

'It's just something that comes over me sometimes, and then the people around me had better watch out. It would be best if I went to sleep.'

That's what I said, but I only wanted to get rid of him because I was afraid that this merrymaking and drinking of his had to do with the proposal. I was afraid too that he would torture me with words about Magdalena as soon as he opened his mouth.

'Pity you don't want to listen to me,' he said, 'and you'd rather go to sleep.'

'And what would you like to say?'

Reeling from the drink, he began:

'Well, you know, the reason I'm toasting is that the proposal was successful. The old gentleman and lady are absolutely thrilled. Zapotočný's the biggest farmer in Leštiny, after all.'

It was if the iron bridge I'd been standing on a while ago had collapsed underneath me. That was how this news affected me, for all that I'd been prepared.

'Well, and what have you gone so pale for?' He peered at my face. You look like your shoes are pinching.'

And while I was still completely unable to take this reality in, he continued:

'She's a bit doubtful, but she'll get used to it. Every woman till now has got used to it. See, she'll be the farmer's wife on a big holding. Such good fortune isn't easily come by. And still, she wouldn't have been very willing if her mother and father hadn't been in favour. And especially the mother. She's as merry as if she hadn't a care in the world. She did all the speaking for Magdalena and she spoke the last 'yes' on her behalf. And she did well, with girls you have to watch out. Last year Magdalena's friend ran away with some tramp. They needed to hurry up with the match, because this girl too might have done the same, according to the mother, and the family would be dropped in a puddle.'

'Do you think,' I broke in, because this concerned me too, 'do you think Magdalena doesn't have the right to decide her own future, by herself?'

'And what should she decide when there isn't anyone better anywhere around? Do you know what it means, brother, to be wife of the biggest farmer in the village?'

To anger him, because this chatter of his was jabbing me in the heart, I said:

'If I were a girl, I'd choose according to my heart and my honour. I'd admire the upright spirit and not the moneybags.'

'You're some sort of a tramp too,' he yelled at me, 'if you talk like that! How can some tatterdemalion be an honest man?'

And when I goaded him with a few more words, he became so furious that he flung both glasses down on the ground, since I was attacking the very principle of the good match they were celebrating.

I let him alone for a while, fuming, and then, as if nothing had happened I asked him to bring me to some place where I could sleep till morning.

While making up his mind to do me this friendly service, he angrily muttered several times:

'You're some sort of tramp too. You're some sort of tramp too.'

We didn't want to bother the Maliariks now when they were inundated with work. Somewhere the woodshed Greguš found two horse-cloths, and I lay down on those in the hayloft. I tell you, even on such a bed I was going to sleep soundly and then tomorrow go off again into the wide world.

Greguš began talking to me again. But I sent him away with the words:

'Brother, tomorrow the sun'll shine, but now I'm desperately tired.'

'And from what?' Groping his way down the ladder, he roared with mocking laughter at my sorrow, which wearied me more than if I'd been chopping beeches since the dawn.

*

It was in vain that I closed my eyes, with a burden upon me like the Deluge that once rolled over the earth. For a long time I tossed about and dug my nails into my palms, feeling how miserably I'd let myself be gulled. I had uselessly counted on the purity and depth of my love. Along with that I'd have needed the second half of the Leštiny common, if I was to match Zapotočný. And that was the most important part of the package.

Though I knew how my situation was now, I wanted to have still greater certainty. That imperative drove me out of the hayloft and under Magdalena's window.

She was lying on the bed as before, but I saw that she was no longer ill. She was certainly capable of sitting up or walking.

Zapotočný was alone with her in the room and at that moment he was giving her a tumbler to clink with him. She did not refuse, but I could see how her tears were falling. A wonder I did not smash the windowpanes and vault in, such was the pain corroding my body.

They drank the toast and Zapotočný put the glasses down on the table.

Licking the corners of his mouth, he sat down at the bedside and bent low over Magdalena's face. He said something to her in a continuous mutter and then went to bolt the door. I heard him gabbling to her that he had to be certain and it would be like an advance payment. Otherwise he would not believe her. He was going to quench the lamp too, but then he changed his mind. He caught both Magdalena's hands, kicked away the stool and rolled onto the bed.

So I had come at the most opportune time. It was not in vain that I'd had no rest in the loft. I did not want to interfere in things prematurely, but I was clear about one thing: I would not let her be injured. As I observed this action by Zapotočný, instead of my one closed fist I clenched them both.

'I'm telling you, brother, that's not done,' I said to myself, and I was about to smash the window.

Fortunately, just then someone tried a key in the door. Zapotočný wasn't bothered, since it was bolted. But with all her strength she tore her hands from his, and the freed hands shot out again and hit him in the face. The blow was certainly a good one, because immediately Jano began to bleed. The movements of the key were repeated. Magdalena wanted to call out, but he placed his hand on her mouth and himself called:

'Who's that?'

'It's me,' said a woman's voice, and I knew it was the mother's.

'Are you by yourself?' Zapotočný asked, raising himself from the bed and wiping off the blood with a hand-towel.

'All by myself, my son,' she said.

He opened up.

She was appalled when she saw him all bloody. But he quickly calmed her down by saying that he'd fallen over on the stool. And indeed, the overturned stool convinced her of that. He added that he'd bolted the door in case anyone found him like that and suspected he'd been drinking more than he could hold.

The mother heard him indulgently and then brought him off to the kitchen to wash himself clean.

No sooner had they left than Magdalena jumped up and herself drew the bolt. With disgust she put the bloody quilt on the chairs and flung herself desperately on the bare bed. She pressed her face to the sheet and she cried in a way that made blood drip from my heart.

I knocked twice on the windowpanes, but she did not hear me. And it was better that she did not respond, because that was no convenient time for an encounter between us. I considered it more prudent to wait till the next day, even though every minute amounted to an eternity.

But now I had no reason to hurry. I was certain that the bolted door would protect Magdalena till morning and that she would not unbolt it for anyone. Then, in the morning, with God's help, I'd begin a new day and complete my duties. I was convinced that any kind of effort on my part to change the course of events would be futile. But maybe through Magdalena's will, there might still be some redemption and salvation. She knew I was there and she would know the next day also where she could find me.

'You know, Magdalena, you must wish,' I whispered, as I departed from the spot under her window, 'you must wish and then I will know what to do. Even now I could break the window and carry you away. But your cousin, Jožko Greguš from Vyšný Kubín, told me yesterday evening that you needed to be watched, in case you ran away with some tramp. And so I do not want to defile your honour. You must not run away, and I must not be just a tramp. I believe, my Magdalena, that we are destined to — and that we will — belong to each other, but we must wait until our time comes.'

With that, I went back to the loft, lay down in the hay, and threw the horse cloth over me.

Through a crack in the roof a single star was looking down on me. She was trying to smile at me, but the smile meant little. Though I gazed at her, I was thinking of that other one whom I had left weeping in her room. I thought of her and, together with her, I thought of all the world's pines and all the sunbeams God had given mankind from the beginning. I thought of all the peaks and valleys through which we could have walked together. I thought of all the towns and villages that we might have passed through, light-hearted and happy. I thought of all the days and years that we would have filled with our life together and with all that was ordained for us.

But after these thoughts my spirits were overcome with a feeling of futility, and, seeking relief, I dug my face into the fresh hay. Its smell was strong and intoxicating, so that suddenly I began to fall asleep. My thoughts faded away and scattered. Everything around me went away, and only the scent of the hay remained, telling me I had Magdalena beside me, that we were sleeping together under the pines in a moonlit valley and those two giant peaks were guarding us. And one of them is called Choč.

II.

I came into the inn to say farewell to Maliarik, because there was nothing more I could hope for.

When I stopped by the bar counter he happened to be filling glasses. I had to wait a while, since a large number of customers had gathered and he was hardly able to keep up with serving them. Sweat was flowing down his forehead and his face was all steamed up and gleaming.

I didn't know what to do with myself while waiting, having no desire to drink. Luckily I discovered a rolled ball of bread amidst the glasses and I took it and started rolling it about some more. While performing this silent work I thought of my own torment and of Magdalena, who would become Zapotočný's wife, as Sarah became the wife of Abraham, Rebecca the wife of Isaac, Rachel the wife of Jacob, and Bathsheba the wife of David. All of them had gone through life, or would go through life, in couples. Only I would wander onwards alone, because she who ought to belong to me was attached by error to another. I would have corrected that error if I had been capable of killing, since it was only by his death that Zapotočný could be overcome. But I would not lay a hand even on him. I would rather bear my agony and ask God to help me live through it.

What joy would there be in gaining Magdalena, if at the same time my soul was encumbered by the remorse and the sin of killing a human being? Better to give up my delusions and continue on my way. Since Magdalena had, of her own free will, decided on her future and pledged herself to Jano, I could not compel her against her will to marry me.

Now at least I knew what I should do, so I had no need to tarry there any longer, making my heart bleed by being near her.

I came up to the counter and gave my hand to Maliarik, who was for a moment clear of his work.

'What is it, Peter,' he asked me, surprised, 'do you want to leave just when the best time is coming?'

'I do, uncle,' I nodded, feeling that the words were cutting holes in my throat. 'I've done all I had to do here and I've no more work.'

'But stay for today at least,' he said, holding me. 'The Saint John's bonfires will be lit tonight on the peaks, and all of us are going to see them. Magdalena won't want you to go.'

'How can Magdalena want me to stay?' the words escaped from my mouth full-voiced. 'How can she want me here, when she has Zapotočný?'

'You see, you grew up together from when you were little,' he explained, 'and people don't forget that.'

'Indeed, people don't forget that!' I repeated furiously, and, to wash away the bitterness that was soaking into my tongue, I ordered a tot of liquor.

I swallowed it with difficulty, like eating an apple core, and when I put the empty glass back on the counter I had no intention of delaying further. Again I offered my hand to Maliarik in farewell.

'So you're really going?'

'Really, uncle.'

Once again he put pressure on me to wait. He enthused about the evening. A bonfire would be blazing on every hill. Himself, he always loved to watch it. As if the sky was burning from all those fires.

Suddenly he stopped speaking and looked at me closely, indicating that he was leaving something else unspoken, something more important for me, and eventually he leaned over confidentially to whisper in my ear.

I too bent my head eagerly towards his lips, because I thought he might have some secret message for me from Magdalena. But the bait Maliarik wanted to use for luring me was this, that there would be plenty of pretty girls and I would be able to take my pick. He avowed that he had always thought I would marry their Magdalena, but nothing could be done now, because she was going with Zapotočný.

I drew back from him as if a snake had bitten me and turned my head out towards the inn. Although it was packed, I did not see anyone, and although the very walls were quivering from the noise, I did not hear a single word. I had only one thought: that I must not stay there even a minute more.

*

I was just making my move, when a young man stood up from a table. He was a sharp-looking, dandyish fellow with a thin black moustache, and, in his sharp, dandyish way, he raised a tumbler, drained it, and called out:

'To you and your three chestnut horses!'

I didn't know him, but he obliged me to drink a toast with him and dragged me down onto a chair at his table.

I'd surely be surprised, he began, that he knew about our three horses. But actually, a little while earlier, Zapotočný had wanted to make a deal with him for one of them. He had seen them all, and the devil alone knew where we'd come by three so identical. My own was the one that he liked best and he'd gladly make a deal for him.

As he spoke Maliarik kept winking at him, and seemed to be giving him eye-signals to hold me there.

I replied:

'Yes, he's a good horse. But he's not mine, because I've only borrowed him and I have to give him back.'

'A pity,' the young man said, 'but even so, we can have a drink together,' and straight away he ordered a litre of wine.

I told him I wasn't going to drink, because I was hurrying to get away from there.

'On account of that Leštiny fellow?' he retorted immediately. 'You're doing the wrong thing. Look at me. I've had no success with her whatever, and I'm making merry for the hell of it. But if I were in your place I'd jump over Zapotočný's head, horse and all.'

Impishly he stroked his moustache and smiled at me agreeably. He seemed a nice fellow but I didn't know what he wanted from me. Several times I looked at Maliarik, but he seemed to be just happy that I was sitting there and not leaving.

'And what would you suggest I do?' I enquired.

Briefly he described to me how Zapotočný was drinking in the county town and telling everybody in turn how he'd had success with his wooing. He was bragging that I and this lad with the moustache wanted Magdalena too, just as he himself did, but Magdalena knew what she was doing. She wasn't going to choose the riffraff when she had the chance to choose a rich man. And so, before long, Magdalena would be his and we could lick our paws. Let the tramp marry a tramp-woman! He was shouting things like that, guffawing at his own words and smashing glasses.

'You see,' the young man said, 'that's the kind of fellow they gave her to. Zapotočný mentioned your name with his snout frothing with hatred, so I came over on purpose to have a look at you. For quite a while there I was watching you with Maliarik at the counter, and I must confess you make a good impression. To prove it, I'll say this: though where Magdalena's concerned I'm a jealous hound, I'd be happy if she was yours.'

His bantering manner made me smile:

'A bit late now, brother of mine,' and I thought of what had happened yesterday.

'Don't talk like that,' he almost shouted at me, 'for a man with courage it's never too late. In your place I'd fight the devil himself, let alone Zapotočný. Actually, if I had to choose between the pair of them, I think without hesitation I'd give her to the devil. That's how much I detest the fellow. And don't you believe that Magdalena chose him out of love. Her mother forced her. If it wasn't for that, she'd have chosen one of us.'

He smiled in his dandyish way and a moment later added:

'And since you're the better man, I'd give preference to you.'

'Are you just trying to tickle me under the nose with a straw?' I asked him, and by now I too was a little more cheerful. 'If so, I could do the same to you.'

'Thanks,' he chuckled. 'Better to have another glass of wine.'

He raised his, we clinked, and we drank.

'So then,' he started in again, 'and now I'll tell you the most important thing.'

He too now tried to persuade me that I should stay till the night, for the St. John's bonfires. Magdalena would be there with the other young people and I'd have a chance to talk to her. By our united efforts we must free her from a situation where she was suffocating, like someone buried in a landslide.

As he spoke, I again remembered her tears the day before and how she had fled to hide in the granary. But what truly overwhelmed me was that look of hers, the last look she gave me when they were sending me out of the room before Zapotočný made his proposal. With that look she had asked me to save her. And instead of that I had gone out, woebegone, into the darkness, like a sheep straying into a furze-brake. I was helpless then because it had all come about so unexpectedly. But when I thought of that now, my breast swelled up, as if I was about to crush somebody. God forbid that it should happen all over again, because this time I would pound everything to dust. That look of hers challenged and incited me to battle. All the more so, perhaps, because this lad with the moustache had brought me to my senses. He was right when he said that for a man with courage it was never too late. I didn't need to kill Zapotočný. It would be enough, even now, if I was able just to speak to Magdalena on her own.

'So then, what are you going to do?' he asked me, raking his moustache with a finger.

'Looks like I'm staying,' I told him finally.

For joy he ordered a new litre and called Maliarik over to drink with us, giving him to understand that we'd made a deal on the horses. While Maliarik was bringing the bottle, the lad said:

'So it's OK ... That bear is filing his teeth for her in vain.'

*

The hills made the whole region look as if it was covered in waves, like a sea. We were waiting beneath one of them for everyone to assemble, so that we could all climb it together and light a bonfire to St. John.

A river trailed through the valley, with lush grassy banks. As it flowed, it glittered against the sky, which that evening had the shape and colour of a tin bowl. Down at the bottom lay a cast-off moon, like a golden ducat.

I was sitting under the trees on my own and listening to the mountain humming behind my back. There was a group of young people on the meadow in front of me, with Jožko Greguš and Jan Zapotočný among them. I thought that the lad with the moustache would be here too, but I couldn't see him anywhere.

By now we were waiting only for Magdalena. She was the only one missing. My eyes scoured the surroundings, alert and eager for her to appear. Without her this evening had no meaning for me; without her all of the Saint John's bonfires were senseless.

I observed that Zapotočný too was annoyed by her absence and he was having to restrain himself before the others, not to let his anger explode. I knew that he wouldn't be able to keep control of himself for very long, because he wasn't entirely sober.

After a while, when the others too had reached the limit of their patience and begun slowly going off up the hill in little groups, Zapotočný said:

'I don't know what that one is thinking of. I've had enough of her shilly-shallying. She's getting my back up.'

'But look, she'll come,' Greguš tried to calm him down. 'She's taking time to doll herself up because she wants to please you.'

'Or someone else,' Jano muttered, looking at me. 'Even though she's made her choice, I have my suspicions that she's still prowling after someone else.'

Jožko begged him to be quiet, not to do her an unwarranted injury, and not to talk such nonsense in front of strangers. This attempt at calming him only enraged him more and I thought he was going to leap out of his own skin with anger. Finally, Greguš took him by the arm and led him away from the others towards me.

Standing right in front of me Zapotočný said:

'But she won't deceive me; I know how to get the better of her by intelligence. I've worked out a way to make sure.'

'And what are you planning?' Greguš asked him.

'That's my business. But she'll soon know that I'm not someone she can lead by the nose, like Moses bringing the Jews through the desert.'

He snorted and a spark flashed in his eyes.

Not knowing what to say next, he pulled out his strongest card and started boasting about his property. Most of all he babbled about his money, finishing up with this:

'You see, I could choose any one I wanted... and she... But I won't put up with it for long.'

Neither of us said anything.

He carried on talking about his wealth and about all the girls in the region who were hanging on his neck. Finally, he turned away from us to face those of the others who were still lingering behind, and said:

'La-la, there are beautiful girls here too. I could have any one of them, because everyone knows who Zapotočný is. If you don't believe me, I'll prove it.'

He was already heading over in their direction, but Greguš tried to hold him back.

'So let her come when she wants,' he thundered, 'because I swear to God Almighty, I'll swap her for someone else.'

Once again he took a look over the meadows, and when he was certain that Magdalena was not coming he could no longer be restrained. He went back to those who were waiting and selected the girl who really was the prettiest. I felt that she was pleased to be distinguished in this way by Zapotočný. In his drunken state he began paying court to her, and his manner towards her was such that the others too slowly began taking themselves off.

Finally we were left there on our own.

Neither Greguš nor I could look on at Jano's playacting, and so we went across to the spruce copse where our horses were tethered. We had both taken them with us from the Maliariks' place, as neither of us had any intention of returning there. After the bonfire was lit we both planned finally to go our separate ways.

In the meantime Magdalena had arrived with her friend, who was Jožko Greguš's fiancée. Jožko gave a start and immediately went over to them. Magdalena was looking for someone, nervously.

I emerged from the spruces and our eyes met. I saw that her face lit up and she seemed to change completely.

When Zapotočný saw her, he began to embrace the girl he was with. He was obviously doing it to make Magdalena jealous, since, I thought, he was having difficulty making it look convincing.

We had to be on our way after the others, and when Jano's frolic with the girl showed no signs of concluding, Greguš called to him to go right away, because we were late.

'We'll catch up with them easily on the horses,' he replied in a lively manner, raising himself from where he'd been sitting with his companion under a bush.

Jano was the first to jump on his horse, and, though we all expected him to put Magdalena up behind him, he gave a hand to the girl he'd been having fun with. Greguš did likewise for Magdalena's friend, and we two, Magdalena and I, I confess, we were left there, standing rather helplessly.

Then Zapotočný shouted, smiling with twisted lips:

'And you two standing there like pillars!'

Magdalena was gazing into the darkness with a pained look on her face, because certainly she was hurt by Jano's behaviour, so inappropriate after the proposal the day before. But then, when I seated her on my horse, I noticed her expression had changed to a quiet look of happiness. As for me, I was quite overwhelmed with joy that things had turned out this way.

As we set off, the first flames shot out on the summit of the hill and grew into a golden column. By that time fires were blazing also on the other heights of the common, and looking across the mountain, they seemed to be held captive by the trees.

*

We were making our way towards the wood.

Though Jano had declared he would lead us, he ordered Jožko to go first, we two were in the middle, and he was last.

The explanation for this arrangement seemed to be that he wanted to hide his own carrying-on, while at the same time keeping an eye on Magdalena.

We went in silence, with just the sound of the horses' hooves, now clinking, now crackling, now pounding, according to the ground. Apart from that we could hear nothing else, because the mountain was silent. But when we moved in deep among the trees the girl who had gone with Zapotočný gave the sort of cry one hears when someone has been pinched. We could also distinguish the sound of kissing and playful whispering during embraces.

None of us turned round. Greguš too was continuing upwards on his horse, with his companion. She was a pleasant, decent girl – as one would expect, because Magdalena wouldn't have chosen just anyone as her friend. And Jožko behaved properly towards her too. That much one could see at a glance.

All of the carryings-on of the pair behind us reached my ears, but I didn't turn round.

I was holding the horse's bridle with both hands and Magdalena was sitting between my elbows. Every time the horse stepped into a hollow or onto a hump, my arms brushed against her hips. With each abrupt movement of the horse we would again come in contact. We said nothing, because we seemed unable to speak. My throat was entirely clogged up with excitement and the fact that all at once I had her so close to me. I could not see her eyes, with their bewitching tenderness. But I could touch and feel her arms, as she held them pressed to the horse's back so as not to fall.

We were climbing more steeply up the hill and the path was becoming steadily more arduous. I noticed that she was seated insecurely, so I offered her some help.

'Magdalena,' I said in a muffled voice, as if the Adam's apple had leapt into my throat, 'Magdalena, you can catch hold of me so as not to fall; it's very steep here.'

Instead of taking hold of me, she reached out for the horse's mane and pressed against the back of his neck. After a moment I heard subdued weeping.

'Magdalena,' I said urgently, 'Magdalena,' but she did not answer me.

She nestled still closer towards the animal's head and grew silent. But her shoulders continued to shake and they signalled how greatly she was suffering. I reasoned it was because of Zapotočný. But I was still unclear whether it was because she had to marry him, or because, on the very first day after the proposal, he was behaving so badly.

I did not want to be kept waiting any longer. Now that I finally had her so near, I wanted to find out everything from her. At the same time I had to be careful, because Zapotočný was behind my back. Just as I was reflecting on this, suddenly I fancied I could no longer hear the steps of his horse behind us. I ventured to look back, and indeed, so absorbed had I been in my thoughts, I had not even noticed that we had lost him somewhere.

I called to Greguš:

'Janko's left behind!'

We halted the horses and checked the immediate surrounding area, as far as we could see. He had turned aside a little way from the path and, at the moment when we spotted him, he jumped off his horse and then gave his companion a hand down.

'Let's go,' Jožko said when he saw what was happening, and both of us understood immediately that our presence at their frolicking would not be wanted.

But this was hugely to my advantage. I no longer had my worst enemy behind me – actually Magdalena's enemy, but I considered him mine also, since I considered Magdalena as mine.

Greguš, who was out in front, would not be able to see anything either, and so I nerved myself to bend over so close to Magdalena that I breathed my warm breath right onto her dress, and I called her by her name.

I called out:

'Magdalena!'

But she did not move.

I waited, and a million times I uttered her name within me. I breathed upon her back and I saw by the moonlight how the fibres of her dress were straining. I saw her shoulderblades and her throat, how it peeped out through the ringlets. I saw her hair, which in this white light took on a yet paler colour. Paler than linen threads. And finally I saw her hands, gripping the horse's mane.

I could not hold myself back any longer. Letting go the reins, I caught her in my arms. That movement expressed everything I had held back the previous evening and night. Although I was holding her and I felt her in my arms, somehow it seemed an impossibility, as if I had torn from the sky that star I had seen through a crack in the shingle. I was holding her firmly, but I was afraid to press her against me. For Magdalena belonged to someone else and I had not yet heard from her lips that she wished to belong to me.

"Why don't you say it to me, Magdalena?" I thought, "why don't you say it to me now, when there's time to do so? In a moment, maybe, it'll be too late yet again."

She trembled, and her shoulders and elbows were cold. I ran my hands over them right to her fingertips, whispering incessantly: "Magdalena, Magdalena, Magdalena". My voice was sinking deeper and deeper into me, like someone falling into a snowdrift. What was it that always happened to me in her presence? When I saw Zapotočný with her I had been filled with a hard, manly courage and I had been capable of carrying her off amidst the peaks and making her my wife. And now, when I was on my own with her, I turned soft, melting away like a sugar cube under dripping water.

I was back again where I had been the day before. Nothing in my situation had changed. Maybe nothing in my situation would ever change.

Magdalena! Magdalena!

*

I always say that events in life are connected like links on a chain.

When I felt so wretched and powerless that nothing could possibly be worse, my horse suddenly pricked up his ears. Greguš's horse too stamped, and both of them stood still. Without warning, a roebuck ran across the path in front of us. Against the moonlight it looked like something that had been shot out of a gun. It was so unexpected that our horses took fright. Jožko's was the first to bound from the spot and start racing like a crazy thing. My own took flight behind him. I was only just able to catch the bridle with one hand and Magdalena with the other. Twigs were snapping beneath us as we flew along.

I was shouting 'Whoa-ho-ho; whoa-ho!' but there was no stopping that horse. He was hurtling onwards at full speed and I had no idea where he was headed. In the end even Greguš was out of sight and it was in vain that I called to him. All my efforts were devoted to somehow getting the horse to calm down.

At last, racing through the trees and the thickets, he arrived in a clearing. I pulled on the reins to try to stop him. He began to buck and rear up with his forefeet in the air. Standing only on his hind legs, he seemed to be dancing with the moon as partner. He whinnied to the sky and shook his insubordinate head. We two on his back were scarcely able to keep a grip, but there was nothing else we could do.

Finally, he calmed down and stood on all four legs. I quickly turned him about, turned him in the direction where I wanted to go, and dug my spurs into his sides. And I shouted to Magdalena to hold on. Then we flew off like possessed lunatics.

Magdalena leaned in close against me, since she had no other option. At that time I still didn't know what I was going to do. For the moment I just wanted to get rid of the other two and be alone with her myself.

We galloped across a good part of the mountain before coming to a foothill, with a stream flowing underneath. It shone with a silver colour, like a fish with glittering scales. We raced down the bank and leaped clear across the water. From there, going straight ahead, we were climbing up to another peak.

The one thing I found strange was that Magdalena did not ask where we were going. That she was not curious about why this was happening. That she calmly accepted it all and did not demand an explanation.

We quickly reached this summit also and, coming down to the brow of the hill, I stopped the horse. I patted him on the neck and loosened the reins. He was wheezing but no longer panicky. He scrabbled with his hooves while once again I took Magdalena in both arms. Here I had no fear of my actions. Here I was certain that we were alone. Here I had no doubt that apart from God there was no one else present. And the presence of God could not bring us any harm.

Thus reassured, I held Magdalena in my embrace, and showing her the valley, which was flooded with light as if it was noonday, I said:

'Magdalena, do you see that valley?'

She nodded and looked in my eyes. Her look might well have weakened me, like the vertigo one has above an abyss. But now I was determined that nothing would keep me back.

I asked her again in a firm voice:

'Do you see that valley?' and I made my confession: 'All this past night I have been looking at it and wishing

I could be there with you when you made your solemn pledge, that you would be mine forever.'

Astonished, she looked at me and wanted to jump off the horse.

'Are you afraid, Magdalena?' I asked her and locked her in my arms, so that she could not leave me.

A moment later I added:

'Don't be afraid, you need not be afraid of me. I won't harm you. I want you to see the difference between me and him.'

I don't know if she believed me then, but when I mentioned 'him' she straightened up and looked all round. She focused her eyes keenly and listened hard. I knew she was afraid he would find us there.

'He stayed below, where the forest begins,' I told her encouragingly. 'He can't find us. This peak belongs to us only and guards us from all evil.'

But even now she was silent, rigid, as she listened to the murmur of the mountain. She had some sort of terror constantly on her face, and in the moonlight she looked like someone dead. I could not bear her agony any longer, so I drew her close to me and cried:

'You don't need to be afraid of anyone any more.'

To show her my strength, I embraced her powerfully, but to show her that I was also kind and good, I embraced her tenderly. She must really have sensed that from my arms, because for the first time she rested against me willingly and slowly succumbed to my embrace. Lightly and deliberately she pressed in on my chest, like a pail entering a deep well.

I understood what this resolution of hers meant, and so, halted there with my horse on the very crest of the peak, I asked God for his blessing. It came to us in the form of the moonlight, which blended into the warmth of the night, filling us entirely.

We had no further reason to remain where we were. I pulled on the reins and made the horse gallop into the pines. As we pushed our way through the dense protruding twigs they smacked us from both sides, but in such blows we felt the grace of inseparability.

I stopped the horse where the mountain had the densest growth. I jumped down first into the thick moss and then helped her down also. Then I tethered the horse to a tree and carried her under a pine-tree.

There we were hidden from the world, so much so that another in my position could have acted the scoundrel and abused her. He could have wound her round his finger with words. He could have confused her with high-sounding promises. He could have bound her to him forever by making her surrender. He could have decided upon any plan whatever, if he knew women well.

I did not want any of that. My intentions with Magdalena were honourable and earnest, because her future was important to me. For what kind of a man would I be if I saved her from one scoundrel and afterwards behaved to her like a scoundrel myself? I would have to despise myself and hide from the light and from the face of God, like those two who were present when the world began in Paradise. And I loved God and the light, because I loved thoughts that were pure and clear.

I set her down under the pine tree on the moss, just to persuade her of my good intentions, so that she would believe me and not be afraid of what I was about to say.

Because there was not much time, I bent over her and spoke simply and boldly, regardless of what the consequences might be:

'I know you are unhappy, Magdalena, and so I would like to make you happy, because you deserve that. Remember our childhood, and you won't have any doubts about me. All women like you, who are beautiful and innocent, deserve to be happy. And because apart from being pure you are also good and tender, I want to find a corner in the world for you, where all your qualities would be loved and none of them abused. Just say, Magdalena, if that is what you want too, since nothing I want matters if you don't want it too.'

After these words she seemed as if she was waking from a dream, unable straightaway to understand the things around her.

So I took pains to repeat what I had said and to make everything still plainer. It was only then that she looked at me steadily and asked:

'Do you know what your name is?'

I was puzzled by this odd question.

'Peter! You know that. Or have you forgotten?'

'Peter,' she repeated hesitantly after me.

I asked her what she meant by this.

'I am afraid,' she replied, 'that it might be like the one in the Bible.'

'What do you mean, Magdalena?'

'That Peter might betray me, before dawn breaks and the wakening cocks crow from their yards. I'm afraid of that, even though I'm not a timid person.'

'How can I convince you?' I whispered to her face, observing how her hair trembled when I breathed on it.

'How can I convince you?' I repeated after a while, because she did not answer.

Finally she began:

'Maybe you think I want you to tell me you love me. But don't expect that. You're a handsome fellow, and you know the things men can say so beautifully, to seduce women. And so I wouldn't believe even the loveliest things. But...'

She fell silent.

'So what do you want from me?'

She spoke at length about our childhood. She spoke fluently and sadly. She spoke of those little boyish deeds of mine that had become engraved in her memory and which no one could ever erase. She told me about her domineering, ambitious and hard-working mother. She told me also that, although she had indeed been promised to Zapotočný yesterday, it was only her mother who had promised her.

She said that it made no difference where a person lived who was suffering, and she would not refuse to marry Zapotočný; but only if it was clear that the person for whom she had locked her heart from others had come to detest her. She admitted that she used to think about me in solitude, longing for me to arrive. She admitted that she often spoke to her father about the incident when I climbed up the icy tree in winter to give

73

grain to the birds and then fell down and broke my arm. I was lying there with my arm broken, and she was watching. When she pitied me, it seems I said: 'That's nothing, the main thing is that the little birds won't die of hunger.' As if in a fever, she had carried those words with her ever since; she thought that there was no better person in the world.

When she finished, she hesitated, which forced me to ask her:

'Perhaps you've been disappointed?'

'I'm not saying that, Peter. But I don't feel sure. We have lived for many years without each other. A person's nature changes. I knew you as a boy, but I don't know you as you are now.'

'You're right, and I don't blame you for being careful. I can't persuade you with words, because you don't trust words. You decide what I should do. I have never thought of any other woman except you, Magdalena, just remember that. I am not thinking of anyone now, except you. I don't want any other, I won't have any other till death.'

She then spoke so simply and openly, with such nobility and courage, that my mind was forced out of its bounds, because I had never heard a woman speak like this before.

'You'll go to your native region, and you will no longer tramp all over the world. With a heart like yours you are not meant to be a vagabond. You'll go to Turiec and you'll take up farming. When you have become a man for whom all those qualities of mine would be worth something, and when you've secured a little corner where I could safely shelter with all these qualities, then come back. I will wait for you, and then I will believe you.'

'Magdalena,' I shouted with joy, leaning over her body, and stars shone in my eyes, as many as in the sky.

She stopped me:

'I haven't said everything.'

I urged her to say the rest.

'I will wait for you, unmarried and pure, even if it takes a year, two, three.'

'Magdalena,' I whispered, drunk with these words of hers, and like a man without a care in the world I inhaled the scent of moss and the scent of pitch and the scent of the pines, which the wind carried over her body. Then I also caught the scent of her body and the scent of the wind.

I bent down low over her. I bent down like a thirsty person over a well in the field. But deliberately I told myself that, if I controlled myself and did not injure her, God would guard her for me until the time I acquired a farm in Turiec and came for her. I believed then that I would achieve this through simple self-denial. And therefore, just bending over her, I looked with desiring eyes into her eyes and at that moment I tasted all of that future pleasure, when we would share what legitimately belongs between husband and wife.

*

As soon as we finished speaking, Magdalena became uneasy again. She was constantly straining and making me look all round, to check there was no-one there. I had to get up several times and assure her that her fears were needless. Once I too had the feeling that there was someone in the bushes right behind our backs. But I laughed at myself, thinking I was just affected by Magdalena's fear.

Granted, it was possible that Zapotočný might have tracked us down. That he might be lying in wait for us here, until we made our way back. He could hide among the thickest pines, which simultaneously protected both him and us. We might not have heard his footsteps with the galloping and stamping of our horse. But I thought it was ridiculous to worry about such things.

This time too I returned to Magdalena with the assurance that she could rest easy, when suddenly a horse whinnied not far away and in my astonishment I was not able to judge immediately how near it was.

Magdalena looked at me wide-eyed, and I saw fear on her face, like the fear of death.

I knelt down towards her and wanted to stroke her hair, to soothe her. My palm was right over her forehead when the neighing of the horse was repeated. I listened intently, but Magdalena grabbed the collar of my jacket in both hands and pulled me towards her.

'What else do you want to tell me, Magdalena?' I asked, because I saw by the set of her lips that she wanted to say something.

'Now we have to part, Peter, but when the time is right we will see each other again.'

'Yes, Magdalena.'

'I will wait for you and I will put off the wedding with Zapotočný by whatever means I can.'

'Good, Magdalena.'

'Do not forget what we've promised each other.'

'I swear, Magdalena.'

She asked me then never to reveal how we stood with regard to each other, not by a single word, because if we were betrayed they would force her to marry Zapotočný. We would trust each other, and this trust would unite us and prevent us from going astray.

'When I return, how will I let you know?' because we hadn't thought about that. She fell into thought, and for the first time she smiled happily. Her smile rested upon my horse. Then she looked again at my face, and said in a tone that brooked no further discussion:

'You will return with three chestnut horses, and the place where you tether them, that's where we will meet. That will be the sign.'

Her firm decisiveness swept me away, and at that moment, for her sake, I would instantly have leaped into fire. Or I would have grabbed an axe and felled half the trees on that mountain. I'd have lopped the spruce trees and carted them off to my moonlit valley. Then I'd have broken stones and laid the foundations for a house. On the stone foundations I'd have built wooden walls and bought tiles in the village for the roof. I would have thrown myself into the work immediately, but that made no sense here, because this region menaced us with many dangers. I had to go off to my native region, as she'd said so wisely and with such conviction. So then, I would go there, and when I had achieved everything that she demanded, I would return. And I vowed, bending over her, that I would be constant in everything and

I would return with three chestnut horses, which would be the sign for our meeting again.

Understanding all this, I swore once again on my honour, and she released my jacket collar. Her hands fell to her hips like ripe apples that have performed their duty and have nothing more to do on the apple tree.

*

In the meantime my horse had been scraping the ground with his hooves and baring the pine tree roots under the thick layer of moss. As Magdalena's hands dropped and we stopped speaking, he too stopped his scrabbling.

Perfect quiet reigned around us. Only the imperceptible murmur of the wind passed through the still depths of the mountains. Not a branch was stirring, or so I thought, and yet I raised my head suspiciously and looked towards the thicket behind our backs, because there seemed to be some sort of shadow flickering there.

I leaped up, and Magdalena too understood immediately. I raced in between the low pines that formed this thicket. Despite Magdalena calling to me to come back, I continued headlong and after several bounds came to a halt in the bushes. Though the moon was shining, in that place it was dark.

But even in the darkness my sharp eyes distinguished a man moving sideways in front of me, and I saw how his hand glinted. I knew him instantly by that clumsy movement and the big paw-like hand in which he held an open knife. It was Zapotočný.

When I moved to follow him, he roared:

'Don't come here, because I'll kill you!'

Magdalena screamed and my horse whinnied.

That confused him a little and he wasn't quick to recover his bearings. He hid his face behind the branches, but it was too late, because I had recognised him. Of the thoughts flying about in my head there was just a single one I could grasp: he'd been lurking there the whole time and he'd heard every word of our conversation. I had no time to think of anything else, because he was raising his hand and pointing the knife at my breast.

'Throw that down!' I shouted back at him.

He did not obey and rushed at me in rabid fury. First I sidestepped him so as not to be hit. Then I nimbly flung myself on his arm, and we both fell into the pine growth. As we were wrestling there I saw Magdalena above us and again I registered Zapotočný's glance, which was fixed on her. He made another attempt to overpower me. I felt that if I released him he would make not for me but for Magdalena.

I therefore shouted:

'Magdalena, go away!'

She did not go. She bent still lower and Zapotočný spat in her face, calling her a name that is given to loose women.

My blood boiled. I knew how morally pure Magdalena was, and so I flung myself upon him like a man possessed. First I knocked the knife out of his hand and then, pinning him down with my knee, I squeezed his throat.

I was scarcely able to restrain myself from strangling him. But I did not want to kill him. I only wanted to disable him temporarily, so that we would have time to flee and he would not be able to follow us. And that is what I did.

He lost consciousness, but immediately began to come round again.

'What now?' Magdalena asked, and her voice was without fear.

I had no time to answer. Wordlessly I seated her on the horse, grabbed the reins, and ran amidst the pines in the direction where Zapotočný's horse had been heard neighing. I could not leave him there for his owner to come flying at our heels. I vaulted up on him, and then Magdalena and I went at a gallop towards the meadow below the hill where we had met on our way to the peak, because that was where we were supposed to rejoin the others. And so we flew over tree stumps and dry brush, and everything crackled as if the mountain were splitting. We flew like the wind and mentally I imagined how Zapotočný, when he came to himself, would get on his feet and how he would grope about when he wanted to depart.

*

When Magdalena and I had reached the meadow beneath the mountain and halted our horses, a quiet wind that seemed silvery in the moonlight was blowing through it. The gusts swept the grass south-eastwards, gently riffling the stem-ends. Plants, caught up in this movement, rustled and effervesced like wine being poured. The evening dew, like peas made of glass, turned white on their leaves.

We jumped down from our horses, intending to wait here for the others. But at that moment, looking down, we saw our group beside the river. In ones and twos they had preceded us and left the hill even before we did, not bothering to wait till the last flames of the fire had died down.

We realised immediately that it would not be good if we two rejoined the others after this outing as a couple. We therefore tried to think what we should do.

Both of us reflected for a moment, looking up at the hill, which, with its still blazing bonfire, resembled a burning bush.

Magdalena was first to speak:

'Peter, it would be best if we parted here. You should not meet Zapotočný again. Not just because he might try to kill you, but also in case he starts a quarrel here, in front of all these people, that would give them the opportunity to drag our names all over the county. They would talk about us incessantly, degrade us, and make a big scandal out of it. And we could avoid all that. No one would know we'd been together, and I would feel more at ease waiting till we meet again.'

'If you think it's best like that,' I told her, 'I will agree. But now that I'm sure you don't want to belong to anyone else but me, I'm not afraid of anyone in the world. Up to now I've been behaving like a coward, but that was because I thought I'd already lost you. Now that I know where I stand, I feel I could carry the whole earth on my shoulders, and the sea and the mountains too.'

She smiled very softly, murmuring gently and lovingly as I pronounced this speech. She let go the horse's reins, placed her palms on my temples, and looked into my eyes.

'I believe you, Peter,' she said, 'but before we part, I want to hear you say one last time that you will return.'

'As there is a God above us.'

I said this decisively and embraced her warmly. In that embrace we recalled once again all we had promised each other. And Magdalena admitted to me that if chance had not brought me there, she herself would have gone off to Turiec that summer. Outwardly she would have been casually visiting acquaintances, but in reality she would have come to look for me. It was impossible for her to decide in anyone's favour so long as she did not know my intentions. And she had done well not to betray the voice of her heart.

Once again I plunged my face into her yellow hair, and afterwards I removed her hands from my neck, caught the bridle and leaped onto my horse.

'You really will return, Peter?'

'I swear, Magdalena,' and I spurred the horse to a gallop.

In a moment I heard the piercing whinny of the horse that remained with Magdalena. I looked back, even in full gallop, and I noticed how both of them, Magdalena and the horse, were gazing after me intently.

*

I arrived among the willow saplings and no one even noticed me. But I spotted Jožko Greguš, his companion and some others, relaxing in the valley by the river.

I was glad that Greguš had returned from the mountain before us. Magdalena would at least have a companion. Actually, I had no fears for her. She had plenty of personal courage. I worried a little about how Zapotočný might behave. I could not say that he was a very evil man. He simply was not the man for Magdalena. He had pulled a knife on me in the mountains only because of uncontrollable jealousy – I understood that much. I had a good understanding not only of women but also of men.

Hidden in the bushes, he had overheard our entire plan, but I did not think he would boast about that to anyone. He would keep silent, because in his own way he loved Magdalena and would certainly make a fresh attempt to win her by peaceful means, regarding the incident with me as merely the ill-considered adventure of an inexperienced girl. He would not want to give up on her, and so he could not let her name be soiled with gossip about infidelity, because then he would not be able to have her in his home.

I wondered if he might injure her some other way. Zapotočný was not a brawler, I believed. I gathered that much from his awkwardness. Today was certainly the first time he had taken an open knife in his hand to kill a man. And only blind jealousy had driven him to that. He would never have done such a thing otherwise. The people of Leštiny, after all, are quiet and God-fearing.

Now I could see clearly what he had planned for that trip to the mountain. He had his suspicions of Magdalena and me, and so he deliberately created the circumstances in which we would not be afraid to declare our love openly. He took that young beauty with him just to pull the wool over our eyes. His entire performance with her was pure affectation, to lay a trap for us.

That was why, when we had met earlier, Zapotočný had said menacingly:

'But she won't deceive me; I know how to get the better of her by intelligence. I've worked out a way to make sure.'

Thoughts like these disturbed me as I left Magdalena. I had all too much time and nothing else to occupy my mind. The journey was long and my solitude drove me to a process of constantly mulling things over.

In fact, I had one remaining duty to perform in that region. It brought me to the village where I had borrowed the horse from a farmer. I had to return him and thank the owner heartily for his use. He had done me signal service.

But even more than that, I was grateful to the horse for something else: that he had not brought down his hoof on Magdalena's face when she lay fallen beneath the horses in the stable. For this animal love I stroked him and, fervently, I offered him many words of praise. Then I remembered that I had a sugar lump in my pocket. I gave it to him to swallow, so he would have at least that much reward.

Finally I took my leave of him, and that night I gave him back to the farmer. And that same night I returned to Turiec.

III.

The main thing I had to do was to fulfil the promise I had made to Magdalena. I had to get myself a farm, so that no one could say I was a vagabond. I could not permit her to roam all over the world with me. We needed a home of our own, a yard, a garden of our own, and I was sure the Lord God would help us somehow.

I had saved a little money already, but that was not enough. I didn't yet know how I would come by the rest, because just at that time the wood business had fallen off. The export trade was at a standstill and there wasn't much money to be made from domestic consumers. Large timber firms were going bankrupt one after the other. The mountains remained untouched, though the trees were mature for felling. Loggers, carters and sawmill workers were losing their livelihood. Poverty was overwhelming the uplands; people were emigrating to try to find work.

Those bad times affected me too. I went round a number of factories, but all of them had large supplies of wood and their products were selling badly. Employers were shortening the working time, lowering wages and dismissing workers in stages. Here, then, there were no prospects.

In such a position anyone could have fallen into despair. But I did not allow myself to be downhearted. I was constantly thinking of Magdalena and the promise I had given. She had said she would wait even three years, but that was a very long time. Even just for my own sake I had to shorten it, since I wanted to see her as soon as possible. Maybe she was being excessively cautious insisting that we should not meet in the meantime so as not to give ourselves away. However, I wanted to fulfil this stipulation of hers also. But that meant that I would need to get seriously to work if I wanted to return soon.

Since there were no prospects in the wood business, I was quick to take whatever work was on offer. I tried many possibilities and had many hard experiences. But no difficulty and no obstacles could divert me from my goal. I knew what I wanted and I pursued it with determination.

Finally, a man from somewhere in the south who was buying horses appeared in our region. He wanted a large number of them, and I immediately grasped this opportunity. We made an agreement for delivery of so many head. I made a great effort and was successful in the trade. A new order arrived, and this was repeated a number of times – whether by chance or good fortune. Though I don't believe in chance, or in good fortune either.

I may say that I became rich quickly. Immediately I began thinking of a house with a small garden to begin with and a piece of land later. But trade is a precarious thing. I had come by the money easily, but I soon lost it as easily again.

I had bought several wagon-loads of horses and I was supposed to send them down south. But just then they closed the borders. I was left with the horses on my hands and they caused me a great deal of trouble. It was because of Magdalena that this bothered me most.

But when a man desires something strongly, the Lord God helps him, and when what he wants is good, He helps him twice over.

I did not waste time bemoaning my bad luck, and I did not lose my faith or my appetite for work. I travelled round to several stud-farms, large estates, sugar factories and distilleries, and I even sold horses on a small scale to farmers in the village. It was exhausting work, but I recovered my lost income.

By that stage I had enough money to buy a house. I'd had the option on one for quite some time and I was eager to get it. That house was not in my native village, but the locality was beautiful and a pleasant spot for anyone. Together with the house there was land, but I did not yet have enough money to buy it. Its owner had gone off to the town, to her married daughter. We agreed that for the moment she would rent it out to me and that I would buy it in due course, as opportunity permitted.

When I had my affairs sufficiently in order for Magdalena to have that little corner of her own where she could preserve her good spirits and have something to eat, I decided it was time to set out on my journey.

I sold all my horses, keeping only three beautiful chestnuts. With these three chestnut horses I set off for Orava. I made for that village which was linked by the bridge to the county town.

*

It had taken me over a year to manage all this. Magdalena, after all, was young and did not need to rush into marriage. If she truly loved me, why would she not wait? I was certain that I would find her there and she would welcome me with those tenderly half-closed eyes. That would be the proof that she had not ceased to be mine.

Mentally I could see the inn, with all the tables laid out as before. I saw the yard, full of poultry, and her in the midst of them with the little bucket of corn. She was scattering grain on the stones in generous handfuls. Everything around her was clucking cheerfully. Everything was nestling against her legs, turning to her as to a mother. She too was smiling, apparently in great joy. The sun glittered on her face. It was the beginning of Spring and the weather was warming up. Her yellow hair yellowed still more in the sunlight. Her smile, so full of Spring, was strangely complemented by the soft movement of her eyes. Until now I had only been looking at her through a crack in the boards on the gate. I could hold out no longer, and I rushed into the yard. In her astonishment she dropped the bucket and all the grain in it spilled out.

That is how I imagined our meeting and I looked forward to it all the way from Turiec to Orava. Now there was nothing to prevent her becoming mine. No one would be able to say to her that she had gone off into the world with a tramp.

*

Full of self-confidence, I arrived at the county town.

Everywhere my eyes rested, I was welcomed by things that were well-known to me. The curved street and its houses. The tall roofs with smoking chimneys. Two churches with towers. The railway embankment and the tracks. The slopes with budding trees. And here was the bridge across the river into the neighbouring village.

I was about to turn towards it, when suddenly I saw that God had sent that young lad with the moustache towards me.

From a long way off he gave me his bright and welcoming smile, where nothing was black except only for that narrow moustache.

He gave me his hand, asking:

'Back in these parts?'

I replied:

'Back again,' and my heart pounded, to think that I was so close to Magdalena.

'And what brought you here?' he enquired further.

I pointed over the bridge to the next village.

He hesitated, looked at me significantly, and finally said:

'I don't know what your business there may be, but if it's on Magdalena's account, you'll be taking your trouble in vain.'

I narrowed my eyes and looked at him through the little rift between the lashes. What, I asked myself, was he telling me?

'Yes, my dear sir,' he continued, 'it's incredible, but Magdalena got married. It's more than a year ago now.'

How was it that I did not fall from my saddle there and then? I felt I was having a fit of vertigo, so I clamped my legs to the horse's belly. Even then I was insecure, because a frightful infirmity overwhelmed me.

Despondently I looked at the young man, repeating to myself half-audibly:

'So, she married,' but by no manner of means could I comprehend it.

'Quite so. It was a year ago,' he repeated.

'It was a year ago,' I said again mentally after him, feeling as if someone had squeezed my head in a pair of tongs.

And as though it were a detail I should find quite inconsequential, he added, eyeing the arches of the bridge:

'She married Zapotočný.'

That was a name I did not have the courage to repeat. Something choked me and cut through my throat, like a swallowed fishbone. My tongue rejected it, as if someone were forcing me to chew chaff. I was unable to utter a sound; I simply stared mutely at the young man, whose face had turned sorrowful. He was indicating how he grieved for Magdalena.

Outwardly, perhaps, I held myself with somewhat more fortitude. But in reality my head weighed a hundredweight and my body froze into ice, though it was hardly the time for ice, with the trees budding on all sides and the whole world evolving towards full bloom.

'Doesn't it surprise you?' the lad asked, puzzled.

'There's nothing strange about it,' I said, putting on an act, though the tears all but flooded into my eyes.

'Well, then,' and he offered his hand in farewell.

'And where are you off to?' I asked him, though I had no real interest in the matter.

'I'm going about my business. But believe me, since Magdalena married there's nothing I find pleasure in here. I'd prefer to go somewhere far away, to forget her. To this day I regret not praying for Zapotočný to break his neck. That's how much I hate the fellow, because he attached her to him by force. If I was able to, which I'm not, I'd rip him to pieces.'

I grudged the time it took standing there and listening to him, when my head was full of other thoughts. I gave his hand a hearty squeeze and indicated that I was in a hurry.

By then, indeed, I had nothing more to do in the village beyond the bridge. I had to go in the opposite direction. If he'd asked me where I was going myself, I would have said: first, to the town for a glass of beer.

But he didn't ask, so I drew on the three horses' halters and off we went through the county town to Vyšný Kubín and thence to Leštiny, where Zapotočný had the farm where she was then mistress.

I no longer imagined her with little buckets in her hands. Her smile, too, was obscured from me. All that remained manifest and pure was that half-closing of the eyes.

91

On the way I kept repeating:

'So she married Zapotočný. That promise on the mountain by moonlight was a bit of fun with a light-minded stranger, whose mind could be fuddled with pretty words. That promise on the mountain was a year of persistent work for me, while for her...'

But I stopped there. Nothing in the world could have made me say aloud that she had betrayed her given word. It was plain to my mind that they had forced her, but she didn't have to let herself be forced. I mused, besides, on whether she might have outgrown the effects of love, which might have died away after my departure, so that it was no hardship for her to marry a rich farmer such as Zapotočný. Or did she not believe me? Me, the tramp?

At that, I gritted my teeth and said in a menacing voice over the heads of my three horses:

'Magdalena!'

My horses thought it was a command for them and they shook their manes in confusion, not understanding me.

'Yes, Magdalena,' I repeated, thinking of the house I had made ready for her and the land I had intended to buy for her.

I did not know exactly why I was going to Leštiny. I had no business there. I had no good grounds for going after a married woman. I did not want revenge on her, nor did I want to seduce her. But the more I thrashed out the reasons rationally in my brain, the further I continued advancing.

Slowly I passed through Vyšný Kubín. I knew Jožko Greguš's house there. I looked boldly in through the windows, because surely he was out on the land. So I went on again, further, till I came by the main road to the Leštiny common and then into Leštiny.

*

It's a lovely village. All spread out in a valley around a stream. From afar one can see the church on a height, amidst old lime trees. Nearby, a cemetery with well-spaced graves. Under the height stands a white rectory. On the opposite side of the road there are mansions that belonged to the old aristocracy. Many of them are uninhabited, with holes in the windows and leaking roofs. The other houses are small and low, but clean and cosy. Drains run out from the yards, and dogs guard the buildings.

The village was quiet at that time, as people were working in the fields.

I had no relations here, so I looked for an inn where I could get accommodation. Not long ago I did have an acquaintance here, a farmer by the name of Zapotočný. But at this point we knew each other only as enemies.

Halfway through the village I actually did find a small wooden inn. There I halted with my three chestnut horses. They were the most beautiful horses the world had ever seen. I had deliberately chosen such creatures so as to make it clear that I was no pauper.

I dusted myself down on the steps and went in.

'God give you good day,' I greeted the innkeeper as a Christian man.

'God give,' he thanked me, but he never took his eyes off my animals and I detected something not quite right in his face.

'Should they not be in front of the inn?' I enquired immediately, not to put myself in the wrong.

'That's not it, not at all,' he said, but somewhat timidly.

'So then, what's the matter?' and to cheer him up, I asked him to pour three decilitres of wine.

He poured uncertainly, looking at me and behaving as if the room had been visited not by a regular citizen but by a devil, disguised as one of ours.

After he had finished staring, suddenly he said:

'Ah yes, yes, you'll be the one. That's how he described you: tall, broad shoulders, hard face, thick eyebrows, dark hair and three chestnut horses.'

'What's all that about?' I asked him.

He laid my glass of wine on the table and went to the bar, where he had a wooden tub filled for washing glasses. He took one in his hand, drained off the water and wiped it with a fistful of straw. He stared at me constantly and through the window at my horses.

Since he had deliberately forgotten to reply to my question, I tried him again. I was prepared to keep nagging at him until he softened. I knew that people from the mountains were mistrustful, and so I looked for some convenient way to loosen his tongue and his anxious mind.

'Come on, out with it, innkeeper. I would like to find out who knows me here and who described me so accurately. From what you said I gathered that my presence here surprises you. I don't like to cause unpleasantness for people. If I'm inconvenient, I don't have to stay here. I'll pay and go.'

And I made to rise and pick up my bag.

'It's not that at all.' Anxious to detain me, he dropped the straw into the water. 'This inn is open to everyone.'

'That's what I think too,' I assured him, 'but I don't know how you would feel in my position. You're looking at me with horror-stricken eyes. When I ask you for a drink, you can scarcely pour it for me. You talk in such an odd way about my height, my hair, and my face, and what strikes me as strangest of all is that you bring my horses into it.'

'Forgive me,' he interrupted me, 'but at that first moment I thought I would turn to stone.'

'From what?'

'The village is full of it. Until lately I thought it was just gossip ... But I see now that it's true.'

Though by now I'd guessed what he was talking about, I pretended to be unaware and I said:

'Speak plainly, innkeeper, because I don't understand what you're saying. Don't dangle all this before me like a scrap of bacon in front of a cat. If that's what you're trying to do, I might lose my patience.'

'God forbid,' he said, busy at his tub, 'but these things are awkward, and a person has to be careful before strangers.'

He dried his hands and came over to me.

There were only the two of us in the room so no one could interrupt our conversation. He sat beside me on the bench, apparently so that he wouldn't have to talk loudly. As he began he looked all round to check whether some third party might be listening. He whispered right into my ear, because walls too often have ears.

He began with my chestnut horses and immediately linked them with Zapotočný's name and Magdalena's name. While I could easily have made those connections myself, it was a shock to hear them from him.

I asked him how he knew all that. He told me people had been saying any number of things, and he had often privately wondered about this affair. But it had never bothered him, until once...

'Until once? Be quick about it,' I bullied him.

'Once Jano Zapotočný himself came into the inn...' the·proprietor began.

Once, one afternoon, Jano Zapotočný himself came into the inn. He ordered a decilitre of brandy for Dutch courage. He sat down on a bench, heavy as a log, put his clenched fist up to the measure, gazed sorrowfully at the ground, and rubbed his knuckles continuously on the wood of the table.

'What's wrong with you, Jano?' the innkeeper said, because he knew that when a farmer leaves his work in the afternoon and sits down to brandy, there's some hidden reason behind it.

Without a word, Jano raised his fist and pressed it to his chest. Now he was rubbing his knuckles on his breast, as previously on the wood of the table. Looking at him, it was immediately obvious there was something inside him that he'd like to crush with those knuckles. His dull gaze betrayed how he'd been suppressing whatever it was for a long time, and now he could suppress it no longer. He had come to kill it with brandy.

'What's got hold of you?' the innkeeper asked him, because he would gladly have helped him, whatever his problem was.

He began to mumble something, but he didn't yet have enough courage. To fortify himself he repeated the order:

'Another tot ... and then maybe I'll shake it out of me somehow.'

The innkeeper poured him another tot, but he didn't drink it, because while it was being poured he started talking and then he forgot about it.

'You know, uncle, I'll be talking about Magdalena.' (His mouth twisted as if he was ready to cry.) 'I can't say she's a bad woman. Maybe there's none better under the sun.' (Again his mouth twisted, round to the opposite side.) 'But although I married her, there was a certain other man who muddled her head and her heart. And now when I want her to think of me, she thinks of him. When I want her to love me, she turns away from me. When I want her to be sweet and loving to me – and Magdalena knows how to be sweet and loving – she looks at me without understanding me. And I ... I ...' (He put his head on the edge of the table and wept.) '...I can't take it any more.'

'So it's true after all?' the innkeeper said to him, 'and I was convinced it was only gossiping tongues.'

Zapotočný threw out his hand, wiped his nose and eyes, and his gaze drifted through the room. He had come to ask the innkeeper for a service and he wasn't able to summon up the courage for it. He asked for a new tot and tossed it down his throat at a draught. After that he asked for another, and so it went on until he got properly drunk. In his inebriated condition, hardly able to keep his balance, he blabbed out everything.

*

It began that evening under the pine trees, when Magdalena and I swore fidelity until death. Treacherous as he was by nature, he had overheard everything, hidden among the pines. To this day he was sorry he hadn't stabbed me with his knife. He'd have sat in prison for a few years, but even that would be easier to bear than the dog's life he had now. Immediately the thought flashed in my head that I too could have pressed my fingers a little harder on his windpipe and I'd have freed Magdalena from suffering and humiliation. But I didn't regret letting him live. What would I gain if I killed a man and became a murderer myself? It wasn't in my nature, because I know that the godly paths are elsewhere, and I wanted to walk on godly paths.

Zapotočný asked the innkeeper to let him know if a man with three chestnut horses passed through the village. That would be the man who had besotted Magdalena. That would be the man who had made his life so wretched. And then he could settle his accounts with him.

'So that's how things are, innkeeper?' I said to him when he finished his narrative.

He nodded and indicated he was worried about having told me everything. But I assured him that he would come to no harm. Quite the contrary, I would look out for the chance to do him a good turn. After all, it was a Christian's duty to be on the side of justice. He had no reason to support the ambitions of this violent man, this drunk, because Zapotočný from that time had become a drunk. By the innkeeper's account he was coming in more and more often, so that even he himself was getting worried about it.

'Well, and what about Magdalena?' I plucked up courage to ask after a while, because I felt more curiosity about her than about her husband.

Although I was trying to give the innkeeper an impression of patience and forbearance, in fact I felt like someone sitting on thorns.

'Well, Magdalena ... she has a bitter life with him. Right from the start, there was something in that whole affair that gave you a bad feeling. Rumour has it there was something foul behind it. It's said that Zapotočný took her by force immediately after you left on St. John's Eve, while the fires were still burning on the hilltops. When he returned from the mountain after his fight with you he found her at the edge of the meadow on her own with his horse. She was defenceless and he overpowered her. That same year they forced her to marry him, because she was expecting a child.'

"He took her by force," I repeated mentally after the innkeeper, "by force, and on that very evening after I left for Turiec!"

When I imagined him overpowering someone so pure and innocent, I could not bear to hear more. I undid all the buttons on my jacket, and as if something was choking me, I also undid one on my shirt under my throat.

The innkeeper, shaking his head, continued:

'I'd never yet seen such a sad wedding. She didn't even cry, but she had a face as if someone was choking her with a noose. Right away I said to myself that nothing good could come of it. When once she stepped into his house, no one ever again saw her smile. That seems to be what infuriates Zapotočný most, that she doesn't show him any affection in public. That she always goes about as though she had toothache. As I said, she doesn't weep or wail, she never complains to anyone, she never says anything bad about him to anyone. But when you look at her you can read it from her face, like you read about the sufferings of Christ from the Bible.'

There he stopped.

What he said had left me quite stunned. My eyes were glued to his mouth, and, fixed on that, although he had stopped speaking, I forgot about him. I was looking rapt at his lips, as if they were still continuing the story of Magdalena and her unhappy life.

It was a wonder my heart was not ripped apart, when those words of his struck it. And they struck it like a blacksmith's hammer on the blazing iron. It was a wonder my hands did not set about smashing and breaking everything that lay around me. A wonder that in my bewilderment I did not mistake the innkeeper's throat for Zapotočný's and choke him to death.

In my most cruel grief I did nothing, merely drained my glass to the dregs and helplessly licked the last drop that remained on my tongue.

Into a silence that sent shivers down my spine, and which was ensconced in all corners of the inn, I said abstractedly:

'So that's how things are.'

'Just so,' he said firmly, and asked whether it was clear to me now why he'd been surprised when I entered the inn.

'I understand now,' I nodded, 'even though all sorts of things still have to be made clear.'

Now I understood why he'd never taken his eyes off my horses, which remained standing under the window. He gazed at them and then asked if he could put them in a stable, so that they wouldn't cause any trouble. I answered that he could put them wherever he liked. Indeed, I told myself, mumbling under my breath: let him put them where he liked, what did it matter to me?

*

The innkeeper left.

He left, and when I remained inside alone I could feel the spittle between my teeth turning to acid. That was from distress, but I thought it was from the wine. I squeezed the three-decilitre glass in my hand till only shards of it remained and warm blood flowed along my fingers.

The smell of fresh blood irritated my nostrils, and when I saw that the innkeeper was already leading my horses to the stable, I jumped up and called through the window to stop him. Let him leave the horses there, I said, I would pay him and go.

'And where do you want to go?' he asked.

I thought about what to tell him, though I knew very well what I wanted. I wanted to mount the middle horse and go in front of Ján Zapotočný's gate. I'd bang on it, and if he admitted me to the yard I'd leap on his neck and there, like a wild sparrow-hawk, I would choke him to death for everything he had done to her. To my Magdalena. To my good and gentle Magdalena. To my beautiful and morally upright wife.

'So what about those horses?' he asked again.

I knew I would reply that he should just put them in the stable. I knew I would soften as soon as she came to my mind.

And so it was.

'Just put them in the stable,' I directed him finally.

I said that to him because suddenly all the viciousness had vanished from me. My hands, which at that moment still wanted to murder, were filled with desire for the touch of smooth white things. My eyes, which would not have shrunk at that moment from death, suddenly wanted to look at life, full as the earth in Spring, full as a cornblade in summer, full as an apple tree in autumn.

*

When he returned, he found me sitting by a little mound of fragments from the crushed glass. He said nothing. He understood that I had to vent my feelings on something. Understanding that, he quite calmly let me sit there and set to work stacking the washed glasses on the shelves. He was glad that it only amounted to one broken glass. He must have been praying that Zapotočný wouldn't choose precisely this time to come in for his tot. And he was right, because if we'd met we would certainly have come to blows.

Though I'd made other plans, there are times when a man can't extinguish the blazing fires in his head. I wanted to go directly and simply to Zapotočný, as befits a man, and sort things out with him as quietly as I could. Today, once he knew what was at stake, he would surely give up all this vicious perversity.

I told the innkeeper, who was now sweeping the water that had spilled on the counter into the tub:

'Take care of the horses for me and I'll take a look round the village.'

He looked at me with narrowed eyes.

'And you're not afraid?'

'Of whom?'

'You should look out for Zapotočný. It'd be best if you avoided him.'

'Well, he's just the man I want to meet. We're men and we ought to sort things out in a manly way.

'I've done my duty... I warned you, and my conscience will be clear.'

'You don't need to worry,' and I looked at him with a mild expression, 'just tell me, please, where I can find him.'

Half-willingly, half-unwillingly, he told me where Zapotočný's house was and how I might recognise it. It was the finest-looking house in the row and the yard was down among birch trees. The walls on the building were white, the window frames were painted grey. It was a house such as no one else had and it would catch my eye immediately.

I thanked him and paid straight away for the wine and the broken glass, so that he wouldn't have lost anything on my account if something were to happen after all.

Of course he had my three horses in the stable, but that didn't occur to me until I was on my way. Indeed, soon after that, I thought of the property I had acquired in Turiec. There was no-one to inherit that from me if misfortune really were to strike. I was about to go back and tell him about this too, but instead I just kept going.

I felt him looking at me through the open window. I could feel his gaze on the nape of my neck, which went stiff, and I felt his gaze too on my legs as they moved laboriously forward.

*

It was a year when the Spring seemed to have come quickly, spreading its most lavish colours and most pungent scents. The leaves seemed greener and the flowers brighter. The wind brought a pleasant smell of loose earth from the land, while at the same time, as I made my way onwards, the fragrance of pitch and pine brushwood came from the nearby mountains.

All this was provoking my senses as I made my way up Leštiny. It seemed to be inviting me to stretch myself out somewhere beyond the bounds of the village and give myself up to delight in all the teeming powers of this season. But now I had to deal with things that were much more important.

Going through the village, I could hear the most varied sounds coming from the buildings.

I heard the tripping sound of flails in the haggard. Some farmer, doubtless, was late with his threshing. A pig squealed in one of the yards. Probably they were preparing to kill it. Further up washing bats were rebounding from wooden tables and their sounds carried piercingly through the entire neighbourhood.

Women were doing their washing at the brook. The water beside them was splashing, swirling, straining. All of them had flushed faces and their bare feet on the stones had turned red. One of them was standing in the brook, washing a quilt. Against the current the cloth kept inflating, which was making all of them giggle. After some time, when her arms slackened with laughing, the current swept the quilt away. She leaped after it, and the water swirled under her and slapped around her shoulders. Grabbing the floating quilt, she flung it on the table among the others and then raised her skirt and began to wring it, because it was completely soaked.

It was just at that moment that I appeared from round the corner. She stood up straight and let her skirt fall back into the water. All of them burst out laughing again and their mood became even more high-spirited. They were feeling so lively that as I was passing alongside them one of them deftly grabbed a piece of plaited bed-linen, placed it on the table and came down on it full-force with her washing bat. The water squirted right into my face. But I didn't spoil their good humour. I pulled out a handkerchief, wiped my face and smiled at them without resentment.

Only one of them was at all old, the others were young. As the saying goes, milk was bubbling out of them like saucepans. The folded sleeves and rolled-up skirts revealed healthy, handsome bodies. Merriment sparkled in their eyes, and when I moved on, they looked after me, desiring. Desiring, as if I was a tall deer in the mountains in season.

Someone else in my place might have said: why torment yourself over Magdalena, when at every step there are women to do God's will? And it was true: I might have had anyone else in her stead. But I'm not that sort of man.

*

Among the other houses I picked out Jano Zapotočný's. I stopped before a broad gate that barred access to the yard. The windows were indeed painted grey and the room behind them showed clearly in the light. I could see two beds in it by the wall, separated from each other. There was a table in the centre, covered with an embroidered cloth. Round it there were chairs, with an old-fashioned carved heart on the back of each. A green chest with painted tulips stood in the corner.

What caught my eye was precisely those two beds where Jano and Magdalena Zapotočný slept, and my heart missed a beat. I had two similar beds in my own house. But mine were placed nicely and agreeably beside each other. For the moment I was sleeping in one of them. The second was reserved for my wife. That wife should have been Magdalena, and she should have waited for me in the village by the county town with buckets in her hands. With buckets full of rye. And I wanted her to drop those buckets in surprise when she saw me.

It didn't happen that way – the reality was quite different. And so I had different feelings when I knocked on Zapotočný's gate. No one responded. I knocked once more. And again without result. I rapped on the window-frame too, but everything remained quiet and the entire building continued to bask in the Spring sunlight.

I was sure there was no one at home. But to be quite certain, I asked the first man who went by on the main road.

There were a few men, as a matter of fact, passing by with picks and spades on their shoulders. They were off to repair the road. One of them was consistently lagging behind, stumbling along, as if not able to keep up. He was the one I stopped and questioned.

'The Zapotočnýs ...?' he pondered, pressing his finger to his forehead. 'Aha, now I know, they've been ploughing in Okružiny since morning.'

I told him I'd like very much to talk to Zapotočný. There was something I had to sort out with him.

'We're going that way,' he said, 'so come along with us, because you'll have to wait long into the evening before they come back. They'll only return when it's dark.'

'I won't miss the chance,' and I joined them, because it was indeed a good suggestion.

Those in front had gone a good way ahead, so we hurried after them. I don't know what they were talking about, but they had lively exchanges and they spoke to everyone out in the fields as we passed.

They called out the Christian greeting:

'Lord God, help the work!'

The answer came:

'Lord God, hear!'

Everywhere people were ploughing, harrowing, digging, sowing, planting.

Everywhere was full of people, labouring, industrious, hurrying.

The entire common was like a huge anthill, steaming under the sun. The fragile wisps of Spring mist slithered over the furrows, like intangible threads left over from an Indian summer.

In the midst of all that, we too made our way. Those in front with picks and spades on their shoulders, I and the older man behind.

I knew we were not going to walk in silence and they would try to find out everything about me. I had fashioned a story beforehand about what business I had with Zapotočný and who I was.

And indeed, when I'd scarcely had time to think, he asked me:

'And where are you from?'

'I come,'– and I lied from caution, in case he knew about the man from Turiec and his three horses which were to be a signal for Magdalena, 'I come all the way from Gemer.'

'All the way from Gemer?' he exclaimed, surprised.

'All the way.'

'And why have you come so far? What brought you here?'

I thought about how I could answer this question adroitly.

Those in front of us had stopped and were lighting their pipes. They sheltered the flame in their cupped hands, so that the wind would not blow it out. And so we caught up with them right at the moment when I would have had to answer the old man's question. I thought he would surely forget about it now. But no sooner had we all come together than one of them asked me:

'And yourself, what's your business in our region?'

'He's going to Zapotočný,' the old fellow replied on my behalf.

'So you've come to take a look at that mountain he wants to sell.'

I didn't know Zapotočný wanted to sell a mountain, but since this helping hand had been extended to me I grabbed it and said as if telling plain truth:

'Quite so.'

'That one here in Sedlisky?' someone else butted in.

'That one,' I confirmed, though I'd never even heard of Sedlisky.

'So it's true after all,' a few of them said in sequence.

And afterwards they added that he was selling the mountain Magdalena's parents had asked him to transfer to her before the wedding. At that time he had handed it over willingly, but now he was selling it just so that Magdalena wouldn't get it.

'That man has no idea what he's doing,' they said.

To learn something more about Magdalena, I threw in my oar and asked who she was. They informed me she was Zapotočný's wife. I enquired further about such trivialities as whether she was young and good-looking, although I knew her age precisely and I knew all about her beauty. But I was doing this only to loosen their tongues and gradually draw out all the information they had. They told me she had been beautiful when she came to the farmstead, but by now she was quite ruined. As if she were really not the same person at all.

I wanted to know if that was because of poverty or overwork, and I too livened up, because I sensed that the others were keen to discuss the matter.

According to them, he was such a dreadful man that she was wasting away with him. They grew indignant as they explained it. When he was a young man all the girls had been crazy about him and not a few of them envied Magdalena, but now they saw what a beast he was. The worst thing was that he had begun to drink.

'And I don't know what he's got into his head about those horses,' remarked one man who had been listening quietly thus far.

'About what horses?' My interest was roused immediately.

'Oh, that's a long story,' my older companion, on my right-hand side, said loudly.

And immediately they launched into this tangle of rumour, like old women who live only on gossip. Of course, the innkeeper had already divulged that the village was full of stories. No wonder if men too were pampering their tongues with the sauce that the best female cooks in the village had prepared.

Each one added something, to give me a thorough acquaintance with this unheard-of case.

And they began like this:

At the St. John's Eve bonfires she had become involved with some sort of tramp (that word 'tramp' stung me), who promised her he would return as soon as he had acquired a farm. Mere empty talk, and any of them would have staked his life on it that the fellow would never be seen again. But she, poor creature, was so infatuated that she believed him, and still to that very day she was waiting for him. Or at least people thought she was waiting, because she took no one into her confidence. Some people pitied her, others thought she was bad.

'There you are,' said a man who looked like he had seen much of life. 'I always say that wealth isn't everything. What good does it do him? The wretchedest dog in the village has a better time.'

'Indeed he does,' several others affirmed.

I pointed out to them that I still hadn't heard the story about those horses.

Again, the man at my right anticipated the others:

'They say that the tramp is to come with three chestnut horses and the place where he tethers them is where they are supposed to meet.'

'But I don't believe that either,' another interrupted him. 'Where would a pauper get three horses?'

'You're right.'

'It's easy to turn a pretty head.'

'And an inexperienced one.'

'Now where, by thunder, did he come by that notion?'

'Oho! He was a cunning chap, for sure.'

'That farm was a fine brainwave.'

'I like how he managed to get that bit about the three horses into her head.'

'Well, they know exactly what promises to use to seduce a particular girl.'

And so they carried on.

'Well,' eventually I made bold to intervene in their chatter, 'who knows if one day, after all, that stranger might stop in the village, right in front of Zapotočný's gate?'

'Oh yes, sure, you've it all worked out,' they made fun of me. 'We know what people like that are like.'

I had a thousand more words of all kinds on the tip of my tongue, but I had no interest in persuading them they were wrong. I was more concerned to ensure that I did not in any way betray myself. Deliberately I asked about the mountains, and specifically that mountain of Zapotočný's in Sedlisky. They saw me as a serious buyer and advised me how much I ought to pay for it, because that was how much it was said to be worth. I pretended to be grateful. In this fashion we came to a beech copse where the ways divided.

Those men with their picks and spades went along one road, the old man was taking another, and they sent me on straight ahead over the crest. That way I would come directly upon the Zapotočnýs in Okružiny.

And so we parted.

We parted, but once the others had disappeared behind a rise I called to the old man.

I said, 'I've got some tobacco, you're welcome to it.' When he got back to me, I drew out a package from my pocket and gave it to him to stuff into his pipe. It was aromatic Bulgarian tobacco which that horse dealer had brought me from the south. The old man was mightily pleased.

That's what you have to do if you want to get some information out of people. The thing was, I still didn't know the whole story about the horses, because those fellows hadn't finished it. So I had to try a different tactic, and I managed it successfully. For this packet of tobacco the man told me so much that I began to think he might be making up incredible things just to show me his gratitude.

He told me, for example, that Zapotočný had bought a large number of horses, each one of them of the most dangerous kind. They bit, kicked, and wouldn't submit to being led. Even a courageous man would find it hard to approach them. But Jano compelled Magdalena to feed and water them. They had given her blows all over. It was whispered in the village that he was doing that to punish her for waiting for the man with the three horses.

'And Magdalena?' I asked with a voice crushed by this horror, but I bore myself manfully, so as not to give myself away.

'She bears it all very well and never complains to anyone,' the old man spoke of this as something well-established, puffing on his pipe.

'Poor little thing,' the words slipped out of my mouth, because I was unable to bear the renewed pain silently.

Right then, I invited the farmer to sit down for a while by the side of the path.

Seating himself, he responded to what I had said:

'She is, she is ... indeed she's a wretched poor thing. Maliarik never imagined his daughter would be wed like that. But they say it's the mother's fault. She was straining for wealth, and she has it now.'

I sat mutely, and he continued:

'The worst thing seems to be those horses... She was six months pregnant when one of them injured her. She was left lying in a heap, and the child came prematurely.'

"Magdalena," I groaned in spirit, clenching my hands upon my knees.

'Magdalena,' finally I whispered this name aloud, my head beginning to spin, so that briefly the meadows fused with the mountains or the bare earth, and all colours dissolved into one.

The man was looking at me mistrustfully and wanted to know if I had some connection with Magdalena, whose name I pronounced uncontrollably in such distress. He asked me if I too had a Magdalena.

'I had a ... a mother,' I said, wringing my palms together.

'Well, and...'

'Well, and... she was six months pregnant too when a horse kicked her in the stomach and she miscarried.'

'And with that, maybe, she died?'

'She almost died.'

The fellow, unconvinced, put me through some more interrogation, but I was no longer in a fit state to answer him. I propped my arms upon my knees and covered my face with my palms. Like the hard man that I am, I wept hard and I slapped all my fingers upon my tears. The old man did not see a single teardrop, because my hands concealed all of them. I could hear him contentedly puffing on his pipe. He may have thought I was chafing my face and eyes because of weariness.

Down the path from us a bell was jingling, and I removed my hands from my face. A cart was approaching us laden with bags of seed potatoes, and a young stallion was joyfully gambolling round it. I gazed at this joyful creature and I was aware how much less God had given him than me, and yet he was joy itself. And I too wanted to experience the joy of this creature. Such are the marvels by which God sustains us on our path.

When the cart had gone by, the man interjected:

'But now we'll have to part, or we might be here at sunset. A farmer has no time for chatting on working days.'

I agreed with him, and we shook hands.

He thanked me once more for the tobacco and wished for my Magdalena to bear me another child in place of that first one. He recommended me to buy the mountain in Sedlisky and pointed with his knobbly fingers to the hill-crest behind which lay Okružiny, where I would find the Zapotočnýs.

*

By then I had met many people on the pilgrimage to my Magdalena, and they had told me of nothing but distress, as if they'd all got together to agree a story.

To begin with, there was the young man with the moustache in the county town. I thought what he had told me was the most appalling news possible. Next came the innkeeper in Leštiny. When I'd listened to him, I was convinced that the account he gave me was even more frightful than the earlier report. Finally, this old countryman, for a packet of tobacco, had given me words fit to draw blood. And truly I wondered what else might happen once I arrived on the scene.

Perhaps it was fortunate that the more I was over-come by distress, the greater was the desire I felt to meet Zapotočný. Once again, when I found myself alone, my thoughts became progressively more sober, and once again I reviewed my entire plan. I was clear in my own mind that I would not brawl with him and that I would sort things out with him peacefully if it lay in my power.

I set off through the ploughed land, up the slope.

I had taken only a few steps when suddenly a strong smell of earth was wafted to me, and I stopped for a moment right where I was. The scent of upturned fur-rows overpowered me. It was a warm exhalation from the depths, rising white above the clay. I reflected that this was the very time when my lands in Turiec ought to be awakening under the ploughshare. I burned with an unexpectedly fierce love for them, and I thought that no occupation could be more beautiful than the country-man's work. For the first time in my life I pondered the question, why I had not ceased long ago to roam about the world and instead settled down and acquired a farm. But I knew that a woman had to appear to rouse a love of the earth in me. And she had to be a woman like Magdalena, who made you feel when you looked at her all the tastes and fragrances of country life.

Looking at her hands, you caught the aroma of kneaded bread. Looking at her feet, you sensed the moistness of morning dew on the grass. Looking at her figure, the contours of your native district's common appeared to you in all their splendour. Looking at her mouth, it was mother's milk mixed with the juice of cherries. Looking at her eyes, you softened in their strength and goodness, as the fruitful land softens under the quiet and blessed May rain.

Already I felt certain that Magdalena and the land were inseparable things. Already I felt certain that, as once in the past when looking at Magdalena I had burned with genuine love for a woman for the first time, now also, looking at the furrows, I was burning with genuine love for the earth.

I had a hundred urges to roll up my sleeves there and then and begin tilling it, never to cease to the very end of my life. I would have fastened on it like a leech on a vein and the years till death would have seemed too brief a time for me fully to satisfy my passion. I did not have even a drop of tramp blood left in me. That's how a noble-minded woman can transform you.

A while earlier the old man had said that we shouldn't still be in this place at sunset. Taking his words to heart, I looked at the crest beyond which the

Zapotočnýs were ploughing, and I made my way over it to the other side.

*

I saw them from far off, and I recognised her first.

She was standing between the furrows, holding a horse by the bridle. Zapotočný was standing behind it with a long stick in his hand. There was a broken whipstock thrown on the ground beside him.

Jano was drawing his arm back when I spotted them, and he struck the horse so hard that he bent till his underbelly touched his chest. He did not whinny, but the sound he emitted was like a wail. And that wail of his went right through my heart.

They were ploughing up the rise and the horse did not want to pull. Probably he was one of those that dislike being a draught animal. But then why was Jano taking a horse that was bad for such work? Anyone might think it was only to be able to beat him so that Magdalena would have to look at his torments. I was surprised that outwardly she was calm as she held the bridle, only that her face was full of sorrow.

Jano, as if possessed by madness, thrashed the unfortunate horse so badly that I saw from a distance how bruises as big as sausages were rising on his back. The unfortunate animal quivered and bucked to every side.

I didn't know if I should rush forward to tear the stick from his hand, or if I should return to the village to denounce his cruelty to the animal. With sweat standing out on my forehead, I decided to do nothing impulsively.

But what happened next compelled me without further thought to run towards him.

When the horse, completely exhausted, would not move even under the most painful blows, Zapotočný came round to his head and whacked him twice across the snout. The horse reared high into the air and tore the bridle out of Magdalena's hands. Zapotočný rounded furiously on Magdalena, but she turned away and with great effort caught the reins again.

'Hold him!' he roared, and then, as if he had lost his reason, he began lashing the horse on the mouth, ears and eyes.

The horse bucked and sought safety. He flung himself to the left and back to the right. Magdalena was no longer able to hold him and let go the reins. The horse plunged right over her, tearing the plough out of its furrow. Magdalena remained lying under his belly, and one blow of his hoof would have been enough to kill her.

I knew then what I had to do.

I flew down the headlands. As I raced I could see blood flowing from the horse's snout on all sides. But Zapotočný continued to beat him and gave no heed to the danger that faced his wife.

Whenever I recall that moment, I say a prayer of thanks that Christ Himself was standing then on that ploughland, because without His presence something terrible would have occurred.

Jano was howling so much that he did not hear me rushing towards him. It was only when I came to a halt before him that his eyes rolled upward with surprise. He seemed to regard me only as an apparition, because even then he kept on beating the horse. I tore the stick from his hand and hit him so hard with it that he rolled over in the furrows unconscious. I was afraid he might have broken his neck.

I rushed over to Magdalena and pulled her out from under the horse. It was only now that he broke into a run and galloped through the whole common, plough and all, as if his head were burning. When some men caught him afterwards there was not much left of the plough, he had battered and mangled it so completely.

Of course, Magdalena was my first concern.

For a second time I had freed her from beneath a horse's hooves. For a second time I had taken her in my arms. I had not been expecting a meeting like this. An entire year I'd looked forward to her dropping her corn-buckets with surprise, while happiness flooded her face like a deluge. Time and again I had paused to listen to children playing, and in their cries I had heard her cry of joy. Because I imagined it pure and sincere like the child's.

Instead of all that, I found her helpless and stunned. Instead of welcoming words I had to concern myself with saving her.

Holding her in my embrace, I looked all round. I was hoping to find a well or a stream where I could get some water. Finally I found one under some hazel bushes and I carried her over there. I placed her on the ground, gathered some water in my cupped hands, and poured it on her face.

She came to herself with difficulty, and in a confused state. Once again she was slow to comprehend the things around her, as on that moonlit night under the pine trees. Several times she opened her eyes and shut them again, without noticing me.

Maybe she thought it was Jano who was suddenly so tender to her and she did not care for his tenderness. She didn't know that Jano was lying in a sprawl down among the furrows. To confirm that for myself, I turned round and made sure he wasn't a danger to us.

For a long time she did not recognise me, and finally I spoke to her:

'Magdalena.'

First of all, as if trying to identify a voice that came out of the darkness, she slowly raised her head, and then, seeming to remember, she opened her eyes and looked into my face, which was bent over her.

'Peter,' she said uncertainly, and touched my arms and shoulders, to be certain that I was real.

'Yes, Magdalena,' I assured her. 'I have come as I promised I would.'

At these words my voice seized in my throat and two tears rolled over her eyelashes, tears such as I had never yet seen her weep. I knew we were both finding things difficult, but I had expected that she would reward me at least with a brief smile for the fact that I had made the journey. Quite the contrary. The longer she looked into my eyes, the more lifeless her gaze became, and eventually she raised her eyes, saying:

'Has something happened to him?' and looked all round her.

She was looking for Zapotočný, and to me it was as if someone had fixed my heart on a spit.

'Magdalena,' I said to her reproachfully, 'do you care more for him than for me? Magdalena...'

'I am his wife,' she remarked bitterly, 'and while I am his my duty is with him.'

'He does not deserve it. A while ago I was watching how he tormented you.'

'People tormented Christ also, and He did not cease from loving them.'

'But you're not Christ, Magdalena,' I said, trying to bring her to reason.

'I only follow Him, Peter.'

'You've gone completely mad.' The words burst from my mouth when I heard her give this answer and saw her dull gaze focused down on the furrows, where the flattened Zapotočný lay.

She wanted to rise and go to his assistance.

I held her back, and syllable by syllable I repeated to her that I had come for her. Either she did not understand that, or it did not interest her, because she remained stiffly unresponsive.

I wanted to say something to her, I wanted somehow or other to take her away.

I began telling her hurriedly that I had a house in Turiec and I would have land there also. I had two beds prepared in the room and no one had slept in one of them, because it was waiting for her. In front of the windows we would have a flowering mauve rose and lilac. There was a long row of apple-trees and a long row of plum trees in the garden. Cherries and walnuts grew beside the fences. On some of the trees there were bird-boxes...

'Aren't you listening, Magdalena?' and I realised with astonishment that all my words were vain.

She would not remove her eyes from the ploughland, and turning in the direction of her gaze I saw Jano Zapotočný heaving himself up from the furrows, and he too was having trouble collecting his wits. He stood unsteadily and tried to remember where the well was. In a moment he was making straight in our direction.

'He'll kill you,' Magdalena warned me. 'You shouldn't have come. I'd have held out somehow until death.'

'He can kill me too,' I said resolutely. 'Life is worth nothing to me without you.'

'We'll meet in the next world,' she rebuffed me, 'when our time comes.'

'I want you in this world, Magdalena. I want you here and I will not let myself be killed, if you promise me you'll be my wife when I find a lawful means to that end.'

And already I had leaped to my feet, because Zapotočný was approaching. I stood firmly, feet well apart, and waited with tension in my chest.

Zapotočný came over alongside us and made straight for the well, as if we were not even there. He bent his head down and splashed water over it. It ran in little runnels down his neck and onto his shirt. He moistened his temples especially, and several times he slapped water onto them from his palms. He held a mouthful of water for a long time and again he spat it out, at the same time tossing away what remained in his hands.

By then I thought that everything would end peacefully, when suddenly, as he was bending forward, with both hands he grabbed a stone that was damming the outflow from the spring and raised it as a weapon against me. All I could do was leap aside from Magdalena, so that he wouldn't hit her. I had no means of defence and Magdalena realised that too, because when he made his move to crush me she screamed so piercingly that the echo resounded for a long time afterward through the upland. All I could do was dodge his attack. But my foot slid on the earth, still slippery from Spring rains, when I tried to leap aside again, and as ill-luck would have it, I went sprawling down the bank. Zapotočný raised the stone high, and looking up from the ground I saw he was aiming straight for my head.

He would surely have dealt me a fatal blow if Magdalena hadn't called at the top of her voice for help.

Instantly the first man with a spade appeared on the crest and came racing down. A few more fellows ran behind him. Women, too, who were gathering brushwood on the mountain, left their work in response. I don't know where so many people could have come from all of a sudden, as I hadn't seen anyone in Okružiny till then.

Jano nonetheless flung the stone at me, but his aim now was uncertain and he missed me. The stone bounced on the ploughed ground and came to rest between the furrows.

I picked myself up quickly, so that the people who came to save me did not know what had actually happened.

In fact, Jano put the entire blame for the misfortune on the horse. With great self-possession he explained to

everyone that the animal had bolted during the ploughing. He had knocked me over when I tried to catch him,
and Magdalena had been afraid that the crazed animal
would hurt someone.

With this tale he fobbed them off.

Magdalena was the one who fared worst. She was
shaking like a sapling. Her face turned white and cold.
In the end she was unable even to utter a single word, as
if her tongue had gone wooden.

The women advised that she should be taken home
immediately.

One of the farmers offered his ox-drawn cart, which
was on the road nearby. They took her there and
brought her down to the village.

*

Jano was very much mistaken, though, if he thought he
could cover over Magdalena's cry for help with a subter-
fuge. That same evening the village was full of talk. Everywhere people were saying that the man involved in that
incident at Okružiny was the stranger who had promised
Magdalena he would come for her. The rest of the story
was easily inferred.

The worst thing was that following all this Magdalena
became gravely ill.

I decided I would not leave Leštiny until she recovered. I had to have certainty, and I needed to hear the
final decisive word from her lips. At that time, I felt,
during the ploughing, she had not been able to collect
her thoughts quickly. In the confusion and surprise it

was hard for her to decide on her own fate, which required thorough consideration. Though I know now that even at that moment she had secretly decided upon one single course – to go away with me forever.

Reports of her illness and recovery were brought to me in the inn where I was staying by a scrawny little villager. Each time we conferred I paid him with a decilitre. He loved to drink, so he tried to come in as often as possible. And thus I had news of Magdalena's every breath.

Mind you, these reports were not joyful. Several times, with my own eyes, I saw them bring in a doctor. The general opinion was that Magdalena would not come through. Indeed, one evening she was so bad that all of us in the inn were sitting there, sunk in dejection. No one was drinking, though everyone had a glass in front of him. But it was I who was most bitterly despondent.

Incessantly I was thinking of my farm in Turiec. Incessantly I matched that farm to those words of hers, when she urged me to abandon my roaming round the world and acquire some little place which she could retreat to with all those qualities I loved in her. Now I had that place, and I had lost her once again. That gave me a knot in my throat, and I had a feeling of contantly being suffocated.

I wanted to see her at least one final time, but Zapotočný would not allow it. I could have got in there by force, but I felt it was inappropriate to commit violence with her death approaching. Already I had waited outside their gate, accompanied by the innkeeper's wife, but I was not allowed in. I wanted at least to look at her through the window, but the curtains were carefully drawn. It followed logically that if she were to die they would not even permit me to see the corpse. Already I was tempted by the thought of bribing a gravedigger to open the grave for me in the dead of night. A man in such desperation is capable of the most outrageous acts.

I had just been contemplating this and thinking I wouldn't have any other option, when the little villager came running in. All pale and alarmed, he stammered out his plaintive message: already they had sent for the pastor.

The lads in the inn nodded their heads, indicating that this was to be expected, but I went out after him with a feeling of hope.

I asked him if the pastor might somehow make it possible for me to see her, because God had placed this hopeful thought in my mind.

The villager readily brought me to the pastor's house.

*

We found him still at home.

He greeted me very warmly, gave me a sympathetic hearing and encouraged me in a way that I found deeply moving.

'I myself grieve for Magdalena,' he said, 'she was a good and pious woman.'

Meanwhile he was making his preparations and I stood while waiting for him. Although he was in a hurry, he continued to comfort me, and he revealed that he was the only person in whom Magdalena had confided the details of her onerous life. She had appealed to him to pray for her, and he prayed to God for her daily.

'She was a woman of great and powerful faith,' he said.

Then he took a prayerbook from the table, pressed it to his chest with folded arms, shut his eyes and prayed:

'And may God receive her into His grace. May her spirit find relief in His kingdom. May her suffering be changed there in eternal glory to the joy of joys. May her goodness receive its reward from the Lord. May her reverence and humility shine with the light of the stars in Heaven. May her love and her purity find a place in the immaculate purity of the angels. May her humanity and faith penetrate our hearts, that they may no longer shelter cruelty and godlessness. Amen.'

When he had finished we set off immediately, because he was hurrying to Magdalena so that she could for the last time receive the Lord's Supper. I walked alongside him with the firm steps of an experienced commercial traveller, hoping I would manage to catch at least her final glance.

My eyes were full of tears, provoked by the pastor's prayer. My eyes were full of tears, but even then I could not cry properly. Though I had always been a stalwart fellow, for some time past I'd felt sorrow suffusing me more and more. It was torment beyond torments, and let no one be surprised at that. Without Magdalena it made no sense to go back to my native region. Better to launch myself into the world once more, being received every day in a new town and a new village. With the south calling me from the north and the west calling me from the east. That way I would forget, and I would be roaming till the end of my life. I knew I would suffer all the world's agonies, but I would not end them by slitting my veins with a knife or putting a noose round my throat. I wanted to die as a Christian and come through all the Lord's trials. No burden would be too great for me to endure without murmuring. But I asked God for one thing, that He would guard Magdalena for me in Heaven. That He would let her sow her blessing on mankind from her little buckets. And that I should afterwards find her with those buckets in Heaven, when my time should come.

*

The pastor made a dignified entrance into Zapotočný's dwelling and, still with a quiet, dignified manner, halted in the room where Magdalena lay.

I entered together with him, but immediately I sensed the resentment this evoked among those present.

The room was almost full of people. As I learned later, the nearest relatives of both spouses were there. Of them all I knew only Jano's sister, whom I had seen recently with the doctor. I also knew Jožko Greguš from Vyšný Kubín and Magdalena's parents.

To avoid misunderstanding, the pastor himself pointed to me, saying:

'I brought him here, because it is not right for you to feel enmity at this moment.'

All of them shied away from me as from an evil spirit. Only Greguš and Magdalena's father came forward to offer me their hands.

Magdalena's father gripped me under the armpit and was about to lead me to the patient. But Zapotočný came forward to block his path. Under his cheeks his jaw could be seen working, as he gritted his teeth.

'My son, it isn't right for you,' the pastor said, 'to cause uproar.'

'I give the orders here,' he answered decisively. 'Apart from those who've been invited, no one else is wanted.'

The pastor came between us, outwardly friendly, but I felt a wind stirring in his breast from Zapotočný's harsh words, and he said:

'It is God's will.'

'This is Zapotočný's house, and my will shall be obeyed here, and not God's will,' he retorted.

The pastor blanched at this blasphemous utterance and warned him indignantly that he would not have God's blessing.

'I have enough of everything,' he retorted in anger, 'and it was for Magdalena's sake and not mine that I called you here.'

I saw that the pastor would have preferred to depart from under that roof. And I saw too that Magdalena's father's eyes were inflamed, quite red from grief. I myself had to take a firm grip on myself, lest my self-control fail me.

The pastor finally sat down to Magdalena and performed the office for the dying.

All of us drew back and waited in silence. When the pastor rose from the bedside, again we came forward. We moved almost on tiptoe.

The pastor, departing, said to Zapotočný:

'I don't want to utter reproaches at this time, but it is actually you who killed her.'

Magdalena's mother burst into loud weeping. She tugged at the ends of the scarf that covered her head. She splayed out her fingers and desperately stuffed them into her mouth. Greguš caught hold of her and quieted her.

All the others were gazing sorrowfully at the bed.

Magdalena sharply turned her head to the right, then to the left. She rolled it over the pillows, as if unable to find a place. Suddenly she breathed out strongly, strained upwards, and fell back onto the bedclothes.

I heard her mother cry out, but I took no heed of anyone. I pushed past Zapotočný and rushed to the bedside. She was lying motionless and, it seemed, with just that kind of smile I had imagined she would have when she greeted me in the yard. Her eyes were closed and she was as pale as the wall. Her hands rested cold upon her hips. I felt she had taken her leave of us already. I was obliged to clasp my temples in my palms, as my head seemed about to fly off. Bewildered, I ran my eyes over her face. Finally they settled on her lips, and only then did I realise that they were crimson. Looking at them, I began to be infused with hope that Magdalena was not dead and would not die. For me that colour on her lips was a sign of life and the continuation of life. That was how God let me know. He spoke to me through that red colour on her lips. I believed, and then I heard God commanding me to leave straightaway, so as not to cause a scandal. I rose, unobtrusively took my hat and disappeared into the night.

*

As I left Zapotočný's room, going through the porch to the veranda, the neighing of horses from the stable made me stop.

I quickly considered what I ought to do now. I didn't know if I should go back to the lads in the inn, or roam aimlessly through the village, or sit down somewhere in a garden on an old tree-stump and wait there for the dawn.

The horses whinnied again while I was pondering. I have no idea how it happened, but suddenly I was moving, following those horses' call.

The stable doors were open and a lantern hung on the wall. I went in, but my first step inside provoked alarm among the animals. Perhaps they supposed it was Zapotočný, because once they looked round they quietened down. Fear walked in that door together with Jano, every time he entered.

I knew these were horses of the flatlands, that they kick and bite, but I took the chance of going in between them. Just one of them shied away and plunged round in a circle. The others bore my presence without fear.

Finally I found the horse that had been thrashed in Okružiny. One of his eyes had fallen right out of the socket and he had a great wound on his snout. All over his ribs and his back there were blotches, and his mane was trembling.

Looking at his ears, I recognised immediately that he was the horse that had brought Jano back from Poland. That was certainly why he had maimed him, because he was one of our three chestnut horses. He had beaten him so unmercifully out of hatred for that trio, since they were a symbol of my meeting with Magdalena.

I stroked him, poor devil, on the thigh, and made my way back out.

The dusky Spring sky was hanging low. Weighed down with vapours from the rains, it lay paralysed over the peaks. Wearily it extended behind the backs of the clouds, in which Choč was entirely muffled.

*

I believe that everything that happens happens by the will and grace of God. I believe that it was by the grace of God that the world came into being and the waters were separated from dry land, so that man could live there. I believe that by God's will the light was divided from the darkness and the heavenly bodies shone to the glory of the Lord. I believe that great is His power and He rules over the human heart, just as He rules over the immense world. I believe that He is everywhere present and that He abides in me also. I believe that He is the power of life and death and that I too will prosper by His grace. I believe that He visits His chosen ones with a cross of suffering, and therefore I too accepted this visitation and humbly sustained it. I believe that with a just reward He rewards those who submit to His will without murmuring. And I believe and will believe that what happened happened by His grace.

That night Magdalena did not die.

When I left her I returned to my accommodation in the inn and sat there till dawn on the edge of the bed in my rented room.

The innkeeper's wife came a few times to look in on me and each time she asked if there was anything I wanted. That evening the story had spread all through the village that Magdalena was dying, and so she was worried about me.

'A little black coffee, if you could,' I said to her once.

She had scarcely turned to go when it was on my table.

'Nothing else?' she asked, reaching out to me tenderly with her eyes.

'No, nothing else,' and I thanked her.

'If you wanted anything nonetheless, just knock on the wall here. We're sleeping right next door and I'm a light sleeper. I'll come to you in a jiffy.'

'It's not very nice to tear anyone out of their slumbers,' I told her, 'maybe I'll get by with this.'

'But just knock,' she urged me with a kind and benevolent smile, 'we're used to that, we don't take the night for granted. You know how it is with the innkeeper's trade.'

'I'm grateful to you. But I'd rather just sleep and know nothing.'

Again, maternally, she smiled at me:

'The coffee'll calm you down, maybe you'll get to sleep.'

The coffee remained untouched and I spent the whole night sitting there awake.

Dawn seemed bitter to me, and the light was harsh, cutting into my eyes when it brightened fully. But that light was a bringer of good at least in this, that it softened Magdalena's image in my mind. All night I had seen her rigid, with candles burning round her.

It was morning.

I moved from the edge of the bed and tried to take a first step. My legs were completely numb, and I was chilled through from sitting stiffly all night. I began walking about the room, to warm up a little. The sounds of my footsteps were the first sounds I had heard that day.

Shortly afterwards they opened the bar and the whole house came alive. People were going in and out of the inn and their talk reached me. I wanted to go in among them, but I was deterred by my own face, which frightened me when I saw it in the mirror. I continued walking here and there and I looked through the window at the broad fields of Leštiny, laid out in strips to the crests of the hills.

Among these the body of my beautiful Magdalena would rest. Among these her good heart would dissolve. Among these she would be changed into dust. I saw her under a covering of sods, and how she would want to lift herself and find somewhere else. Let's say, in a summer sunspot on a path through the corn, and for me to be there to pick a tangled cornstalk from her yellow hair. But she was no longer able to decide for herself, because death had deprived her of all power.

'You know, Magdalena, that's how it has to be,' I consoled her, to make it easier for her, 'because all of us come from the sin of Adam and Eve, and so you and I are of dust and to dust you must return.'

I was standing opposite the window, my back to the door, when suddenly someone opened it and came in.

The innkeeper ran up to me with outspread arms, gripped me by the shoulders and shouted in my face:

'She's alive... She's alive... She's alive...'

Uncomprehendingly I gazed at his mouth and I swayed with exhaustion. I had to rub my forehead several times to come to my senses and understand.

'Magdalena?' the word finally came out of my mouth.

'Magdalena,' he confirmed, and then I saw his wife behind him, wiping away tears with her apron.

'What are you crying for?' he asked her. 'You ought to be glad.'

'Oh,' she sobbed out every syllable, 'it's from happiness.'

When I came to myself somewhat, I demanded, just so that I could fully believe in this miracle:

'Who actually told you that Magdalena's alive?'

Then I learned that this message had been brought by the villager who was in my service. They said he had rushed in so overjoyed that he immediately ordered a litre of brandy and was treating everyone who came into the inn on my account – this, allegedly, because of Magdalena's resurrection from the dead.

Although what he did was uncalled-for, I was unable to feel angry with him. I understood that joy is expressed in a different way in each human being. I wouldn't have had any objection if he'd ordered a whole barrel at that moment. After all, to me Magdalena's life was worth the entire world.

Hurriedly I washed and combed my hair, and with hat in hand I went out without delay into the village.

Everyone surely must have thought I was going to Zapotočný, but I went elsewhere. I went to the pastor in his rectory.

*

'Welcome,' he called to me when I was still some way off, and he came towards me.

'Good morning, pastor,' I greeted him.

'What news do you bring me, my son?' and he gripped my hand.

I told him I had very gratifying news.

'And what?' he asked.

As if breathless, I rushed to get the words out:

'Magdalena is alive, pastor.'

At these words the pastor's eyes widened and lit up brightly, he exhaled with delight and almost embraced me. But then his eyes darkened again and his face became grave. I didn't understand this sudden change. He explained it to me with the first sentence he spoke.

And what he said was:

'Actually she would be better off dead, though I know I am causing you pain by saying so.'

'That is precisely why I have come,' I told him, 'so that you as a pastor may advise me and we can decide what should be done.'

137

'And what is your particular concern?' he asked me.

It was impossible that Magdalena's life of torment should start all over again, and therefore I was offering, if I was the cause of her suffering, that even at the price of the greatest agonies I would do whatever was needed so that Magdalena might live as she deserved.

The pastor thought for a moment, laid his books down on the table, and then looked fixedly at me. He was examining me with his gaze, and it seemed he wanted to know if I was really a man of such fortitude that I could bear what he was now about to propose.

I was truly resolved to do everything for Magdalena. When I imagined how she had suffered up to now, I would have let myself be killed right there on the spot if that would have redeemed her. No one could demand a greater sacrifice than that from me, and I was not afraid of it. I was prepared.

He said:

'There is only one solution that would be pleasing to God. We will call Zapotočný and you will declare to him here, on your honour and conscience, that you will depart from this region and that you will never again come back... in short, that you are renouncing Magdalena forever.'

I need not say that at these words it was as if he had sliced right through me with an axe, or as if he were cutting flesh from my body piece by piece. I had to make great efforts to control myself and collect my wits.

What happened to me did not matter. This was about Magdalena.

Eventually, I looked firmly into the pastor's eyes.

'Well, my son?' and he waited for an answer.

With trembling in my heart I answered him:

'Let God's will be done. Let Magdalena be redeemed. And may her happiness be as great as my suffering will be without her.'

The pastor, touched, gave me his hand and squeezed mine as a sign of his satisfaction with my manly and Christian utterance.

At once, he sent the parish clerk for Zapotočný.

I laid down one condition: Zapotočný must promise that he would never again injure Magdalena and that he would live with her as a decent man should.

We had scarcely finished talking about that when the parish clerk returned, alone. Farmer Ján Zapotočný announced that his household was no business of anyone else's and that Magdalena would have the life she deserved.

Wrinkles formed between the pastor's brows. His eyes grew sorrowful and his lips were pressed tight. He took a while before he began to speak. Shaking his head, he said that Jano was a lost man, a completely hopeless case. His deceased parents had been very pious. They would be appalled if they could see him as he was now.

'I wanted what was best,' he told me, 'and I am grateful to you for trusting me. I will not forget that.'

For a while we continued sitting together, but then we were disturbed by parishioners coming in for a christening. Leština's newly-born citizen launched into a wail in his godmother's arms, and we rose.

The pastor asked me not to leave for Turiec as yet. If I could spare a little more time, he would like me to wait.

He hoped Zapotočný would come to his senses and that it would be possible to speak to him reasonably. And if not directly, then he would call Jano's sister, who also had a large farm holding inherited from her parents, and ask her to speak to her brother. She was a good and noble-minded woman, the very reverse of Ján Zapotočný.

Accordingly I left the rectory, but I remained in Leštiny.

*

Magdalena was slowly recovering.

In the county town I sought out the doctor who was treating her, and I besought him to work hard for her return to health.

On that same occasion I encountered the young man with the moustache. I was greatly surprised when he spoke as lucidly about the whole thing as if he had been in Leštiny and right there in Zapotočný's house. He revealed that a particular woman was a regular visitor to his house and that she always had a few words to say about Magdalena.

'As you know, women like to gossip,' he said, smiling, 'about any little thing at all.

I nodded and listened to him further.'

'So you see,' he continued, 'I know all about her. All the time. And about you too, more recently.'

He laughed and, giving his laughter a particular undertone, looked mischievously into my eyes.

I asked him what he knew about me.

'You acted as though it was nothing to you,' he answered, 'and suddenly you're in a fight with Jano in Okružiny.' (Again he examined me with narrowed eyes.) 'But even this very day she's still worth fighting for. Tell me, is she still so beautiful? But I'm surprised at you that you keep tempting her now that she's married. I know, though you didn't tell me, that you loved her even from childhood. You must be a stubborn man, to keep persisting so long. It's the same with me, but only because I'm living so near her. Oh, by the way, in case I forget to tell you: at the end of the month I'm off to the Hungarian border. Give my greetings to Magdalena. A pity that thug got her. If he weren't so watchful, I'd surely have pulled his guts out. You know that he violated Magdalena first of all, to force her to marry him? Basely and violently he overpowered her. It tore the guts out of me when I heard that. He made a good speculation there. Sure enough, she didn't have any other option but to become the spouse of his fortune, to conceal her shame. And then when she was in her sixth month he sent her in among flighty horses. You know that her child was born prematurely? What a scoundrel!'

'I know,' and acknowledging this, his indignation seized me also.

'He's an inhuman scoundrel,' and he trembled with anger, 'to do such harm to such beauty!'

He grew thoughtful and fell silent. He was looking along the county town square, where puddles of water between paving stones threw back the light. Stubbing his toe on a stone as he walked, he played with it with the tip of his shoe. I sensed immediately that somehow he had been tamed and his fighting spirit was not what it had been. And I noticed too that his wit had lost its

141

sharpness, though even now he would still catch fire and make his jokes.

'Something's bothering you,' I said, disturbing him in his musing.

'You've guessed right,' and he looked at me sharply.

'May I know what your trouble is?'

'Everything,' came the evasive reply.

'Maybe you ought to trust me, maybe I deserve that.'

'Not very much,' he was choosing his words carefully, 'but if you insist I'll tell you.'

'Just tell me.'

Without further ado he admitted that it was I whom he felt angry with now. He couldn't come to terms with the fact that I was so well able to conceal my feelings, while actually playing the principal role in the whole affair. Even down at the bridge, where we'd met a few days before, I acted as if it didn't interest me. And afterwards all Hell broke loose. He had no notion of what I was planning, but one thing was clear to him now – that all his efforts had ceased to make any sense.

'What efforts?' I asked, intrigued.

'I wanted to help Magdalena ... and now I'm useless to her.'

He wanted to help Magdalena, but he had not supposed that she had me in her heart. That reality had left him quite at a loss. He acknowledged having previously told me that he would wish her to me, but now he was sure the case was otherwise and he had made a mistake. He was only angry at Zapotočný, but he was jealous of me.

I assured him that even the people he was angry with and jealous of didn't have it so easy. Maybe they were suffering twice over. Even Zapotočný was being eaten away and suffering like a man in Hell.

'That's what I wish for him, the villain,' he blew out some air with relish and stroked his moustache, 'may the burning sulphur roast him!'

I told him he shouldn't curse like that. But my advice only agitated him more.

'Do you know what he did yesterday?' he raged, but maintaining a certain smoothness, typical of the townsman.

'You're staying in Leštiny, after all, so you'll certainly know.'

I assured him that I'd left the house early that morning and I didn't have the least notion of anything.

'Very well, then,' and he began telling the story.

The Leštiny woman who visited him said that Magdalena had gathered her strength sufficiently to come out to the yard, the front of the house and the garden. Though even now she never said a bad word about her husband, people somehow knew everything. Some uninvited ears had been listening when she complained to the pastor that she couldn't even move, because Jano saw an evil purpose in every movement she made. She'd hoped his disposition would improve after that near-fatal illness of hers. But he had begun his outrageous treatment of the horses again. The animals knew his footstep by now and they trembled even when he was still far off. Even he couldn't approach them now on his own. That very night the one he'd been beating in Okružiny broke loose and ran away. The night watchman caught him and brought him back. Zapotočný suspected

Magdalena of having untied him, and that this was another prearranged sign with that tramp.

'Forgive me,' he apologised, 'for calling you a tramp, but that's the word I was told Zapotočný used.'

'No need to ask pardon,' I said, at pains to be friendly. 'I don't take offence at a little thing like that, so long as nothing worse happens to me.'

He gave me a strained smile and ran his fingers through his moustache, which always sat above his upper lip like a bradawl.

Our conversation was faltering since we seemed to have no more to say. Otherwise, this young man, as it happened, had done me a great service with a few words, and for the second time. It was particularly important for me to have learned what had happened that night.

In gratitude I squeezed the young man's hand four times on parting and wished him the healing of all his wounds at his new posting close to the Hungarian border.

So then, the old story with the horses was continuing.

It was clear that Zapotočný was by now so addicted to his vices that nothing would tear him free from them, neither love nor menaces. But that meant it was once more necessary to keep watch over Magdalena and her life.

I hurried out of the county town and decided that I would not go a step beyond Leštiny but keep vigil over her. I also resolved to pay an immediate visit to the pastor. Sooner or later an end must be put to Jano's excesses. Magdalena could not possibly be left in such a hopeless position. If there was no other way, then it would be necessary to speak to her parents and ask them to take her home. I believed this was something the pastor could do as a last resort.

*

Several days went by.

A calendar with large black numbers was hanging on the wall of the inn. I used to consult it and count out on my fingers how long I had been away from Turiec. The sound of the pendulum clock reminded me that the farm I had bought was awaiting my attention and I would have to go back to it.

The innkeeper's wife swabbed the windows, wiping away the traces of rain.

The innkeeper went to put out some oats for my three horses, who were impatiently awaiting my departure. They were like prisoners, continually in the stable - even though we did groom them a few times and let them out in the yard to run around. But I know they were not happy without work.

That day there was a fair in the county town.

No sooner had the woman wiped the windows and closed them than a large group of men piled into the inn. I helped to carry glasses while we waited for the innkeeper to return. These men had come from the fair and wanted something to clear their throats. Sitting behind the tables, they laid out their bags containing lunches they hadn't yet eaten. The inn was full of the smell of sausage and good smoked bacon.

'Come and taste some of ours,' one man called out to me, and I recognised him as one of the group of road repairers I had met on the way to the Zapotočnýs at Okružiny.

I cut myself a slice of sausage, so as not to offend them.

'Have some bread too,' he pressed me.

I cut a slice of bread too.

'It's good,' they all avowed, 'because it's from the rye on our own lands.'

And all of them, as if to order, praised the good soil of Orava. I knew that it couldn't be compared with the soil of Turiec, but I let them have their pleasure. Indeed, to gratify them I declared that I liked their common. If I didn't have a farm in Turiec, I said, I would immediately settle here.

'You have a farm?' asked one of them in surprise, and a second and third.

'Indeed I do, like any one of you.'

I observed how the expressions on their faces changed after I spoke these words. In conversation with me they were immediately more open and friendly, once I had presented myself as a farmer and when they no longer needed to believe all those yarns about vagabond-ism. Now I understood quite clearly how poor a thing is the soul of a tramp compared to the soul of the farmer.

I was no tramp, as a matter of fact. I simply factored wood and for that I was obliged to go about the country. But from the time when I decided on another life, on the farming life, I would have wanted to stay on my own headland and wait there till the wind had blown right through the blood and bone in me, till the smell of the earth had permeated me completely, so that no one could ever distinguish the wanderer in me again. What I wished for myself was that everyone looking at me would see the farmer, a thousand years turning and moulding the good peasant earth.

When we had talked our fill about our commons, one of them for a change pulled a floral scarf out of his knapsack, so he could boast of what he had bought for his wife. He pressed it upon me to have a good look and asked me if the women in Turiec wore anything so beautiful.

I was just reaching for it when we heard a scream in the village.

All that time I was like someone walking on needles. A tiny rustle was enough; my ears had been sharpened.

Now I said to the lads:

'There's something going on outside. Do you hear it?

One of them smiled and waved his hand:

'It's a custom of ours that the girls pour water on young men when they're leaving the ploughing. Some-one has surely got a bucketful. You'd better be careful yourself.'

'Yes indeed, women's wiles,' another added.

But some of us got up and went out in front of the inn. From there we could see Ján Zapotočný's sister running, and she was calling out for help for the love of God and for the wounds of Christ.

I ran over to her, disturbed by a strange intuition. The others came along behind me.

'What's going on?' I asked her.

'Just come, I beg you,' and she wrung her hands.

All of us rushed up the village. We had no idea where it would take us. But when we approached Zapotočný's house, a powerful stink of burnt horsehair or horses' hooves wafted down to us. A clinking of chains was coming from his yard, a clatter of feet and a horse squealing.

We broke into a run.

Zapotočný had a horse standing in the middle of his yard. It was the one from Okružiny, with his empty eye-socket and his gashed snout. Magdalena was holding him with a chain, all pale and with a tortured face. She was very weak and didn't at all have the strength needed, because the hand gripping the chain was being jerked this way and that by the horse. Zapotočný had presumably dragged her straight from her bed to torment her with the animal's suffering. Putting this together with what the young man with the moustache had said, that lately the horse had broken loose at night and that Jano suspected Magdalena of setting him free, then everything was clear.

Zapotočný was burning a word on the side of the horse's belly with a red-hot poker: T-r-a-m-p.

He had heated the poker under a boiler that was placed near the well, where normally pig-feed was heated. Now there was a fire in it, sputtering and crackling.

When the poker was blood-red with a white-hot tip, he pulled it out and kicked the oven door shut. Winding a rag around it, he brought it over to the horse.

Sweat was rolling down Jano's forehead and temples. Everything in his appearance strongly suggested that these excesses were products of a state where constant mental pain was passing over into madness.

We had just run up to the gate when he took the fiery poker to the horse, which was already shying and trembling. First of all he stopped, holding it over the branded letters. He scrutinised them: in places they were burnt right into the flesh. Apparently he was satisfied with them, because then he turned towards the horse's head.

I was the first to grab the handle of the gate, but I discovered it was locked, which made the horror still worse.

'I'll run home for an axe,' I heard behind me.

That would be good, since we'd have to cut through the boards. Strong iron bands were holding them, so they couldn't be kicked in. Someone suggested breaking the windows in the house and getting in that way. I was attempting to climb up on top of the gate, to launch myself into the courtyard from there.

'Don't be a fool,' someone behind me pulled me back. 'Don't tackle him on your own, he'll kill you too.'

'Better wait for the axe,' another advised.

In the meantime the number of curious onlookers had increased and they were standing all round the front of the house. The tremulous weeping of Jano's sister came piercingly through the hubbub of the crowd.

Zapotočný began to raise the hand with the poker.

I wasn't sure if he was aiming for Magdalena or the animal. But by then I was ready for anything.

Because the owner of the axe had not yet returned and I could no longer bear waiting, I smashed in a window frame, leaped into the room, and from there rushed into the yard.

I was just coming out the porch when Jano pressed the fiery poker into the horse's second, sound eye.

The horse reared up in agony and screeched in a way that sent horror right through me from head to foot. Then I heard the first blows of the axe on the gate. Idiots, they should have jumped through the window after me, but in the disturbance they lost their reason.

The horse tore free of Magdalena and launched itself with its forefeet as if for a jump. Zapotočný was unable to avoid it. Battered by the animal's hooves, he fell to the ground.

Like a wild being I jumped from the balcony into the yard. But it was too late, I could give no protection now.

Deprived of sight, the horse did not know where to turn. He threw himself backwards once more, and then, scared by the cries of the people in front of the gate, he took flight. Unseeing, he dug his hooves into Zapotočný's breast and slammed an iron shoe into his right temple. At a gallop he ran through the yard towards the garden. He crashed into a stone wall and maimed himself so badly that he had to be shot on the spot.

Although Magdalena was crying out, I turned to Zapotočný first. When I raised him he lay in my arms as limp as a flail, and immediately I knew he was beyond saving. He was motionless and the blood flowed so fast from a wound on his face that it flooded over his eyes.

Later, the coroner's investigation established that he had two ribs broken and another fractured. The blow to his head was fatal. Jano died instantly there and then.

I placed him back on the ground when I saw that he had given up his spirit and nothing more could be done for him.

By now a hole had been cut with the axe and some of the lads had squeezed through. I borrowed the axe and, whacking the locks off the gate and its little door, let them enter freely.

Probably half the village rushed in. The crowd was standing all along the road like a bank of cloud. Jano's sister pushed her way through them, crying desperately for her unhappy brother.

Even I felt a little sorry for him. But I'd wanted to make an agreement with him, hadn't I? I could not have done more than I did, when I resolved to renounce Magdalena forever in the interests of peace and her happiness. But then, how could she have been happy without me? Maybe it was for the best that Zapotočný had not come to the rectory that day. And I believe that he did not come because God had plans for us that were totally different.

*

They buried Zapotočný on the third day.

Of the people who were there at the funeral, all were weeping. Some for Zapotočný, others for Magdalena, and I, quite uniquely, for myself.

I stood in the crowd, looking at the coffin and at Magdalena. When I saw how she grieved for the death of that tyrant, I could not hold back my tears. There, for the first time, I felt freed of duty, like a small child, because for the first time I sensed definitely that I was indeed an intruder. It was possible for me to think that Magdalena had loved her husband after all, when I saw how sincere and deeply-felt tears coursed down her face.

But she did not love him. I became convinced of that later. She wept for him only as an unfortunate, quite as other people did. And she wept too for herself and for her desolate life.

'It won't be like that any more,' I told her tenderly and consolingly, when the pastor and I visited her that same evening in her house.

I sensed, having spoken these words, that she was no longer able to imagine anything beautiful and good. That she found my language alien. That she had entirely forgotten the touch and embrace of my hands. That tenderness to her was like the stirring of a mild breeze, which a roughened face does not feel. That she gave as little weight to the talk of happiness and peace as the inveterate swearer does to the name of God. I felt we were only vexing her with such things.

'You don't seem glad,' said the pastor, 'my daughter, you don't seem glad that we came?'

She was perplexed and unable to give any ready answer.

'Magdalena,' I said, weaving myself into the conversation, 'I want you to decide your future by your own will, now that you are free again.'

'I don't understand what you want from me,' she said finally.

I bent closer towards her across the table, round which we were sitting. I knew that long preambles would be of no use here, so I began right away with the central issue:

'Magdalena, I have a house and I am going to have land too, which I set about acquiring because of you, because you wanted me to have a house and land. I came to this region to seek you, because you wanted me to come. I have done everything I promised you, only now I don't know if you still want to fulfil your promise also.'

'I am Zapotočný's wife,' she said, with a bitter accent on the words.

'I know,' I assured her as calmly as I was able, 'that you *were* Zapotočný's wife, but that is no problem for me.'

'He took me by force when I was single, and we were expecting a child,' deliberately flinging at me the things that might repel me.

'I know that too, Magdalena,' I acknowledged sincerely, 'and I don't understand why it should make me turn against you.'

'Because I told you,' she cried, 'that I would wait for you pure and unstained ... but I couldn't, Peter.' And she burst into tears, 'I couldn't, because they forced me.'

'I know everything, Magdalena, and there's nothing you need apologise for to me.'

I went on to explain to her that we would not keep looking back at the things that had been, but we would fix our attention on what now will be.

And there will be happiness, full and healing, which will soon sprout from the rye sown in the fields at Turiec. It will sprout too from the long tracts of wheat that will sway in the wind. It will bud in the leaves and flowers of the fruit trees that fill the garden. It will bud in ourselves, it will overwhelm us like a river flooding the lands by its banks. And however strong we may be, we will not be able to resist, because that force will be stronger than us. People have learned to call it happiness, but we two, my Magdalena, we will call it life.

That is how I spoke to her, but not because these are words that can make a fine impression and seduce women, as she herself had observed a year and a half previously in the moonlit valley, lying on the soft and spongy moss. No, not for that reason, but because that was how I felt and I was prepared for everything.

I sensed she was yielding a little, in spite of everything.

What I myself could not manage, the pastor achieved. Until then he'd been walking about the room looking casually at the pictures on the walls, without intervening in our dialogue. But when I had finished, he returned to us and helped me to win Magdalena over completely.

She was not so rigid now, her movements showed more warmth. Eventually a feeble smile even spread around her mouth, and all at once it restored her former beauty and her commitment to life.

*

Magdalena's mother did not agree with our course of action. She did not want to allow Magdalena to marry me, and so we were married with two witnesses against her will. After that great tribulation we belonged to each other forever, but I did not wish to take Magdalena to my home until she had become my lawful wife. In this the pastor was extremely helpful, because he had a clear understanding of the law, both human and divine.

We remained only briefly in Leštiny, until the matter of property was sorted out.

Magdalena renounced her inheritance in favour of her former husband's sister. She required only that the two best horses be given to Jožko Greguš of Vyšný Kubín. That was the one desire she expressed in connection with Zapotočný's home.

When we had completed all our duties, we finally set out for Turiec.

So as to avoid any unpleasantness with Magdalena's mother on parting, we decided to go by night across the hills on our three chestnut horses, which were waiting in the innkeeper's stable. By the following morning we would have reached our journey's end.

We said farewell only to the pastor, the innkeeper and Zapotočný's sister, with whom we arranged that everything we needed would be sent on to Magdalena in Turiec by rail. The main thing was that by then we should be there.

We set off for Vyšný Kubín and thence we turned off towards the hills and on further in the direction of Veličná. From Žažkov to Veličná we crossed by ferryboat.

As I said, we went at night.

The darkness of that night was soaked in the heavy moisture of Spring. Under the hooves of our three chestnut horses the earth was steaming and crumbling.

The clouds hung on the stars and sucked at the sky like a child at its mother's nipple. The hills were fragrant with brushwood, because those hills are simply one great brushwood expanse, and they seemed to be raised high against the horizon.

Suffused with the wonder of that silent night and that journey of ours, I suddenly realised why everything around us is so beautiful once we are alone.

It was our first night. It was our wedding night. And the animals that were carrying us seemed to sense that; they were picking their way around stones so as not to jolt and disturb the peace around us. For this I was grateful to them.

But even apart from that, they were immensely precious to me. It was due to them that I was leading Magdalena to my home. It was due to them that Magdalena was sitting alongside me on the back of the middle horse and that now I could say to her, boldly and without fear: my wife. It was due to them that I was holding the bridle with one hand and with the other I could range from Magdalena's shoulders down her arm to the fingertips. I would gladly have continued on to the ends of her big toes and from there to the crown of her head. I would gladly have touched her forehead, her mouth and her eyes. I would gladly have touched each of her limbs and every part of her body, to assure myself once again that all of it now belonged to me and everything was now already mine.

But Magdalena after so much tiring activity was sleeping in my arms and I did not want to wake her. I was glad she was resting and that with me she had found